MANDIE
AND THE
HOLIDAY SURPRISE

Mandie Mysteries

MANDIE
AND THE
HOLIDAY SURPRISE

Lois Gladys Leppard

BETHANY HOUSE PUBLISHERS
MINNEAPOLIS, MINNESOTA 55438

T 27711

Mandie and the Holiday Surprise
Lois Gladys Leppard

Library of Congress Catalog Card Number 88–71502

ISBN 1–55661–036–X

Published by Bethany House Publishers
A Division of Bethany Fellowship, Inc.
6820 Auto Club Road, Minneapolis, Minnesota 55438

Printed in the United States of America

For Shannon Mason Leppard,

My beautiful daughter-in-law,

With Love.

Table of Contents

Chapter 1 / Creature in the Room

Mandie and Celia ran ahead of Uncle Cal as they climbed the stairs in the Misses Heathwood's School for Girls. The flu epidemic was over and it was time to settle down to classes again. Christmas holidays were coming up next, also their quarterly examinations.

"We'll open our door for you, Uncle Cal," Mandie called back to the old Negro man who worked for the school. Stopping at the door, she quickly turned the knob and flung the door open. Then she stood back to allow Uncle Cal to enter with the luggage.

The two girls froze in horror at the scene that greeted them in their room. April Snow was just releasing a mouse from a fruit jar into their chifferobe. The mouse jumped back out and disappeared under the bed.

Mandie and Celia screamed and quickly stepped backward. April Snow darted past them and ran down the long hallway.

Uncle Cal instantly set down the bags he was carrying and crawled around on his hands and knees, looking for the mouse.

Just then Miss Prudence Heathwood appeared in

their doorway. "What's all the commotion about here?" the short, thin headmistress demanded.

"A m-mouse, M-m-miss P-prudence!" Mandie managed to reply.

"What?" The headmistress took a step backward.

. Uncle Cal got up from his hands and knees. "De mouse got away. It done gone," he explained.

"We know exactly who put this one in our room, Miss Prudence," Celia said. "It was April Snow."

Miss Prudence turned to look at the auburn-haired girl. "April Snow? How do you know that?" she asked.

"She was in our room when we opened the door," Mandie explained.

"Yessum," Uncle Cal agreed. "We saw huh puttin' dat mouse in de chifferobe, we did."

Miss Prudence frowned. "Are you sure about this, Uncle Cal?"

"Yessum, we seed huh fo' sure," the old man replied.

"The mouse jumped back out of the chifferobe and ran under the bed," Mandie added.

"I'll see to her," Miss Prudence promised. "Uncle Cal, get the mousetraps and set them in the room. We have to catch the thing."

Celia looked worried. "But what are we going to do, Miss Prudence? We can't stay here with that mouse running loose," she protested.

Miss Prudence thought for a moment. "We don't have any more rooms for students, as y'all know," she replied. "So you have my permission to sleep in the guest room on the first floor until the mouse is caught. But you can't move your things down there. It would be too much clutter."

Mandie and Celia looked at each other.

"Miss Prudence, I know the easiest solution to this problem," Mandie said. "If you would let Uncle Cal go back to my grandmother's house and get my kitten, Snowball, he'd catch that mouse fast."

"A cat in this school?" Miss Prudence exclaimed. "You know I don't allow any animals here."

"But Miss Prudence, we could keep him shut up in our room," Mandie offered. "He wouldn't bother anyone."

"He's a good kitten," Celia added. "He always lets you know when he wants to go outside."

Miss Prudence didn't reply but stood there looking at the two girls.

"Dat cat, he be a good cat," Uncle Cal spoke up. "Missy 'Manda be right. He catch de mouse in no time flat. Be easier than traps. De girls, dey might step on de traps."

Miss Prudence sighed in irritation. "All right, Uncle Cal. Go get the cat. But remember," she said, turning to the girls, "that cat is not to be let out of this room. Do you both understand that? And when he catches the mouse, he is to be sent back to your grandmother's house, Amanda. Do you hear?"

"Yes, ma'am," both girls agreed.

"Thanks, Miss Prudence," Mandie said. She looked over at Uncle Cal, who was setting the girls' luggage inside the room. "Please hurry."

"I be on my way," he replied.

Without saying anything more, Miss Prudence hurried down the hallway.

"Uncle Cal—" Mandie grasped the old man's arm. "Do you think Aunt Phoebe would mind coming up here to help us unpack while you're gone, just in case that mouse shows up again?"

"You jes' wait right heah in de hall," he said. "I sends Phoebe right up."

As the old man started down the hall to find his wife, who also worked for the school, the girls walked over to the windowseat across the hall and sat down.

"Oh, what a terrible thing to happen on our first day back to school!" Celia fussed. "I hope Miss Prudence punishes that April Snow good."

"Don't worry. She will!" Mandie predicted. "I just don't understand why April Snow is always doing mean things to us."

"It is odd how she keeps after us," Celia agreed.

"I think she's just trying to aggravate me, probably because when I first came here, I moved out of her room to move in with you," Mandie said thoughtfully.

"She's only making trouble for herself when she tries to make trouble for us," Celia observed. "And we don't ever do anything back to her."

"I can't let April spoil my excitement," Mandie said, looking out the window. "I'm just so anxious to get back home for Christmas. I want to know what the big surprise is that my mother has for me."

"It must be something awfully important," Celia told her friend. "Otherwise your mother wouldn't have sent Uncle Ned all the way from Franklin to your grandmother's house here in Asheville just to tell you. I'm just glad the flu epidemic is over and we can all get back to school and get this term over with."

"Me, too," Mandie agreed. "But I'm still worried about Hilda. I hope she gets well soon. Grandmother Taft said she would let me know how she is from time to time. Maybe Hilda will get well in time for her and Grandmother to go home with me for Christmas. I wish you could go to my house for Christmas, Celia."

"You know I have to spend Christmas at home. But my mother promised that we'd go to your house in time to see the new year come in. Just think, it'll soon be 1901."

"Yes, 1900 sure went by fast, didn't it?" Mandie replied. "So many things have happened this year."

"I'm not going to give you your Christmas present from me until we come to your house for New Year's," Celia told her.

"That's good because I wanted to wait to give you yours then, too," Mandie said. She drew a deep breath. "Oh, how I wish I knew what my mother's surprise is. I can't even guess what it might be."

Celia jumped up from the windowseat. "Here comes Aunt Phoébe," she said.

The old Negro woman hurried to meet them and embraced them both at the same time.

"I'm glad to see you, Aunt Phoebe," Mandie said. "I'm so happy you and Uncle Cal didn't get the flu."

"Amen, Missy 'Manda," the woman said with a nod. "We been prayin' to de good Lawd to stay well so's we could nurse de sick girls here. Thank de Lawd it's all over and gone away." She glanced over their shoulders. "Now where be dat mouse?" she asked, leading the girls into their room.

"It went under the bed," Mandie answered. "But just wait until Uncle Cal gets back with Snowball. That kitten will find the mouse in no time."

"Meantime we better be gittin' dese heah clothes hung up in de chifferobe," said Aunt Phoebe, bending to pull things out of the luggage where Uncle Cal had left it.

Celia kept looking around on the floor as though she were afraid to move.

"Celia, that mouse is not going to bother us with Aunt Phoebe here," Mandie told her. "Here, let's help do this." She shook out a dress to hang.

Celia began her unpacking but still watched the floor. "Y'all are two smart younguns," the old woman said. "Y'all knows dat mouse is jes' as 'fraid of y'all as you is of him. If you sees him, all you gotta do is shoo at him, and he'll run away."

"But we don't want it to run away," Mandie protested. She hung her parasol on a hook and reached for another dress to hang in the chifferobe. "It'll be here forever if we don't catch it somehow."

"Dat white cat of yours, he gwine to git him, so jes' don't you worry 'bout dat mouse," Aunt Phoebe said, putting the girls' hat boxes on top of the chifferobe. "When you seen dat Injun man what be a friend of yo' departed papa?"

"Uncle Ned?" Mandie replied. "Oh, he was at Grandmother Taft's house yesterday. He brought me a message from my mother that she has a big surprise waiting for me when I come home for Christmas," Mandie said. "But he didn't know what the surprise was. He just left me wondering about it."

Finished with the unpacking, Aunt Phoebe closed the door of the chifferobe. "Well, I reckon you'll see what dat message be when you gits home fo' Christmas," she said.

At that moment Uncle Cal appeared in the doorway with a large basket in his hand. He set it down in front of Mandie. "Heah be dat cat, Missy 'Manda," he said.

Mandie quickly removed the lid on the basket and

grabbed Snowball before he could jump out and run away. She held him close and he purred.

Celia pushed the door closed. "Put him down and let him get that mouse," she said.

Mandie stooped down and gave Snowball a push under the bed. "Go get that mouse, Snowball."

"We'se got to go now," Aunt Phoebe told the girls. "We'se got work to do."

"I got a message from your grandmother, Missy 'Manda," Uncle Cal said. "She say to tell you dat Hilda's up walkin' round."

Mandie stood up and clasped her hands in joy. She looked over at Celia and both girls smiled.

Uncle Cal continued. "Not long after y'all left, Hilda got out of bed."

"Thank the Lord," Mandie said excitedly. "I knew she was going to get well. You say she's well enough to walk around?"

"Dat what Miz Taft tells me to say to you," the old man said, smiling. "She be up and wantin' sumpin' to eat."

"I'm so glad!" Mandie exclaimed.

"She'll probably get to go home with you for Christmas, Mandie," Celia said.

"Thank you, Uncle Cal and Aunt Phoebe," Mandie said.

"Let me know what happens to dat mouse," Uncle Cal told the girls as he and Aunt Phoebe left the room.

The girls hurriedly put away their small things—ribbons, gloves, handkerchiefs, and stockings. Then they took their school books out of their bags.

"We sure didn't get any studying done while we were at your grandmother's, did we?" Celia remarked.

"No, we didn't. I suppose we ought to brush up now

on some of the things we're supposed to know for exams," Mandie answered.

"Right. I need a lot of brushing up," Celia said, rolling her eyes.

Sitting on the windowseat in their room, the two girls reviewed the lessons in their workbooks. Quarterly examinations would start any day now.

The big bell in the back yard of the school started ringing to beckon the students to supper. Making sure the door was tightly closed behind them, Mandie and Celia scurried downstairs to the hallway outside the dining room where the students assembled for meals.

When Aunt Phoebe opened the French doors to the dining room, the girls quietly hurried to their places behind their assigned chairs around the big table.

Miss Prudence came through the doorway on the far side of the room and went to stand at the head of the table. Picking up a small silver bell next to her plate, she rang it to get the students' attention. "Young ladies," she said, "we are so happy to have you all back after that siege with the flu. And we're thankful we didn't have any permanent losses from it."

The girls stood attentively, listening to the headmistress.

"We *have* lost quite a few days from school because of the flu, and now Christmas is almost here," she continued. "Because of this, we will not have time to put on a play for the holidays. However, we have all been invited to Mr. Chadwick's School on Wednesday night for a holiday dinner with his young men."

There was a slight murmur among the girls.

Miss Prudence rang her little silver bell. "Young ladies, please let me finish," she said. "I'm sure you will all want to hear this. We have decided to dismiss you for the holidays on Thursday morning."

Every ear was listening now as the headmistress continued.

"I know we were to have our quarterly exams before Christmas, but we will postpone these until you return after the holidays. We will have classes for review tomorrow morning. I would advise you to study during the holidays and be prepared for examinations when school reopens Monday, January seventh," she said. "Are there any questions?"

The headmistress paused and looked around the room. No one ever dared ask a question of Miss Prudence. She could make a person look foolish. All the girls took their questions to Miss Prudence's sister, Miss Hope. Miss Hope was always ready to listen and to help.

The headmistress spoke again. "One more thing. We are going to do everything possible to get the electric wires and the furnace installed, so that when you return to school we will have electric lights and no further need for fireplaces. The workmen have promised to work while you are away. Are there any questions?"

The girls remained silent and she went on. "We were able to get a Christmas tree put up in the parlor while you were all out because of the flu. However, it has not been decorated. May I have some volunteers to do this? It needs to be done right away because Mr. Chadwick and his boys will come calling on us tomorrow afternoon for tea. Who will volunteer?"

Mandie and Celia looked at each other, and both of them raised their hands. No one else responded.

"Amanda and Celia, thank you," Miss Prudence said.

"The decorations are in boxes in the parlor. Please be sure you two are finished and in your room before curfew at ten o'clock. Young ladies, we will return thanks now and be seated."

After the meal when Mandie and Celia turned to leave the room, they overheard Miss Prudence speaking to April Snow.

"Go straight to your room, April," she said. "Remember, you are allowed out only for classes and meals. And if you break any more rules, the punishment will be severe next time."

April looked at Miss Prudence without saying a word. Then quickly leaving the room, she ran ahead of Mandie and Celia and hurried up the stairs.

"So, April has to stay in her room," Mandie said as she and Celia walked down the hallway to the parlor. "Maybe she won't get a chance to do any more meanness."

"I doubt that she stays in her room," Celia replied.

As the two girls entered the parlor, they gasped at the sight of the beautiful Christmas tree standing in the room.

"It's so tall we can't reach the top to decorate it," Celia said.

"Well, I suppose we'll just have to ask Uncle Cal to help us. He's nice and tall," Mandie said. "Let's see what we have to decorate it with first."

Hurrying over to the boxes nearby, they knelt down and pulled out garlands, ornaments, tinsel, fancy bows, and lots of other beautiful things.

"That tree won't hold all this stuff!" Celia exclaimed.

"We'll pick out what we want and put the rest back in the box," Mandie said, pulling out a streamer. "This is going to be fun. I love to decorate Christmas trees."

"Look at this ball," Celia cried, holding an ornament

up for Mandie to see. "Isn't it pretty?"

As Mandie examined the fragile ball, Snowball peeked out from under the tree to play with the ornament.

"Snowball!" Mandie exclaimed, picking up the white kitten. "How did you get here?"

"You know how," Celia said. "April went upstairs, remember? She probably went into our room again."

Just then Uncle Cal came into the parlor with a stepladder. "Miz Prudence sent me to hep git dis heah tree decorated," he told the girls.

"We were just saying we'd have to ask you to reach the top for us," Mandie replied.

Noticing the kitten Mandie was holding, he said, "I thought dat white cat s'posed to be up in dat room catchin' dat mouse. Did he come down fo' supper, too?"

"Supper? Oh, Uncle Cal, I'm glad you said that. Snowball hasn't had anything to eat since he got here. I forgot all about it," Mandie said.

"While y'all pullin' out dem decorations, I'll take dat cat to de kitchen. Phoebe, she in dere. She feed him good." Uncle Cal reached to take Snowball from Mandie.

"Thanks, Uncle Cal." Mandie gave him the kitten. "Please tell Aunt Phoebe that Snowball is not supposed to be running around loose."

The old man smiled as he left the parlor with the kitten. "I knows," he said.

When Uncle Cal returned, he helped the girls cover the tree with lots of the bright glittery things in the boxes. Finding a huge star, he fastened it to the top of the tree.

There was freshly cut holly lying in a corner, and the three of them fashioned clumps of holly with some of the other decorations and put them around the room.

"Did you hear what Miss Prudence said?" Celia asked

Mandie. "The boys are coming over from Mr. Chadwick's School tomorrow."

"I know. I suppose Tommy Patton will be with them," Mandie replied as she straightened a garland on the tree.

"Are you hoping he will?" Celia asked.

"I suppose it would be nice to see him again," Mandie mused. "Do you hope Robert Rogers will come, too?"

Celia stopped to think. "I don't know, Mandie. He makes me nervous or something when I'm around him. I almost spill things, and I just can't think of anything to say."

"You'll get over it," Mandie assured her friend. "All girls growing up get like that some time or other, I think. After you've been around Robert awhile, you'll get used to him. That's the way I was around Tommy, but when my mother and Uncle John and I went to Charleston to visit his family, I had a good time. I sort of got used to him, I suppose."

"But how long does this 'getting used to' take?" Celia asked. "When you went to Charleston, you were down there for days. I've never been around Robert except a few times at things we do here at the school."

Mandie laughed. "Oh, Celia, the more you see someone, the more comfortable you become around them. They get to be friends with you."

Uncle Cal perched silently on the ladder during this whole conversation, straightening the decorations on the upper part of the tree. "Dat's sho' right, Missy," he said at last. "Takes time to make real friends."

"How much time?" Celia asked.

"Oh, I don't know." The old man laughed. "I'd say by de time dis heah school lets out in de spring, you oughta be knowin' dat Robert fella purty well."

"That is if our school has events that include the boys' school. Otherwise we'd never see Tommy and Robert." Mandie put the extra decorations back in a box. "These are left over, Uncle Cal. I suppose you know what to do with them."

The old man stepped down from the ladder. "I'll take care of them, Missy 'Manda," he said. "I think you girls did a purty job wid dis heah tree."

As the girls stood back and surveyed their work, they agreed.

"We'd better get Snowball now and take him up to our room," Mandie said.

Celia suddenly frowned. "That mouse will still be in our room," she said, "because Snowball hasn't been there to catch it."

"I'm sure he'll catch it tonight," Mandie assured her. "Come on. Let's go. Thanks for helping us, Uncle Cal."

After the girls picked up the kitten from the kitchen, they went to their room. But when they looked around, they found nothing out of order. If April Snow had let Snowball out, evidently that was all she had done.

Leaving Snowball there, they went downstairs to the guest room to sleep. That night Mandie dreamed of the surprise her mother had waiting for her at home. In her dream, the surprise turned out to be a beautiful Christmas tree.

Chapter 2 / Uninvited Guest for Tea

The next day the girls had a hard time concentrating on their review lessons. The talk in general centered around what to wear when the boys came over for tea that afternoon.

After the noon meal, Mandie and Celia looked through their clothes while Snowball prowled around the room. He had not yet caught the mouse, and it had not reappeared.

"What am I going to wear?" Mandie sighed, pushing the hangers apart in their chifferobe.

"What am *I* going to wear?" Celia echoed. She reached over Mandie to help look through their dresses.

Mandie's hand rested on a red velvet dress. "This is it!" she cried. "Red for Christmas."

"I'd save that for dinner tomorrow night," Celia suggested.

"That's a good idea," Mandie said. "Let's see, I'll wear this tan and brown silk dress this afternoon," she decided, pulling it down from the rack.

Celia grasped a gray silk dress by the hanger and took it out of the chifferobe. "I'll put this one on."

Mandie looked from her dress to Celia's and said, "We're going to be a conservative-looking pair with these dresses, aren't we?"

"Yes, but that's the way my mother's friends look for an afternoon tea," Celia replied. "Always plain and simple. Besides, tomorrow night is the time to brighten up and have a party look, don't you think?"

"You're right," Mandie agreed. "But let's wear some jewelry. I think my locket and chain will do."

"And I'll wear my watch on a chain," Celia added as they began dressing for the tea.

Mandie slipped into fresh silk stockings. "I'm glad everything is going to be informal this afternoon and we don't have to have partners," she said.

"Me, too," Celia replied as she stepped into a long taffeta petticoat.

"But don't forget what Miss Prudence said," Mandie reminded her friend. "Tonight the boys are supposed to ask the girls to be their partners at dinner tomorrow night."

"I suppose Tommy Patton will ask you to be his partner," Celia said, fastening the buttons on the waistband of her petticoat.

"Maybe," Mandie answered, fastening her own petticoat around her waist. "I just know Robert will ask you because he is absolutely fascinated by you." She laughed.

Seeing that her friend was teasing, Celia laughed, too. "I suppose I'll have to put up with some boy for dinner, so it would be better if Robert asks me. I haven't even spoken to any of the other boys."

Mandie stepped into her dress, pulled it up, and began buttoning the tiny buttons down the front. Celia pulled hers over her head.

Then they paraded before the full-length mirror, which stood in the corner.

Mandie smoothed the skirt of her dress. "Celia, look!" she exclaimed. "I'm growing! This dress is getting too short for me, and Mother just had it made last summer!"

"Of course you're growing," Celia replied, glancing at her own skirt in the mirror. "I am, too, but it doesn't show yet with this dress." She straightened up and tried to stretch tall. "Maybe a little bit."

Mandie's blue eyes squinted at her image in the mirror. "I guess I *should* be getting taller," she reasoned. "I'll be thirteen years old next June." She tossed back her long blonde hair which she had left loose for the afternoon tea.

"Don't forget, we're about the same age," Celia replied, twirling her long skirt. "I'm going on thirteen, too. And I'm a teeny bit taller than you are." She reached into her dresser drawer to find a ribbon to match her dress and quickly pulled her auburn curls back with the ribbon.

"Tommy is so tall that I have to lean back to look at him," Mandie remarked. "Joe is tall but not that tall."

"Will Joe be at your house for Christmas?" Celia asked.

"He and his parents are all coming," Mandie replied. "Joe's school will be out, too, and his father has to come to Franklin to doctor sick people, so they're going to be staying with us."

"I wonder when your mother will tell you what the surprise is," Celia mused.

"As soon as I get home, I'm going to find out what it is," Mandie said quickly. "I don't know why Mother couldn't have just told Uncle Ned so he could tell me."

"Be sure and find out before I get there so you can tell me," Celia urged.

Snowball suddenly leaped through the air. The girls froze, staring at him. Then they breathed a sigh of relief. He was only playing.

"Whew! I just knew he had caught the mouse!" Mandie exclaimed.

"Me, too. Maybe he'll catch it while we aren't in the room."

"I don't imagine April Snow is being allowed to go downstairs for the tea," Mandie said.

Celia frowned. "With all of us downstairs she'll have a chance to come back into our room here."

"But if she does any more meanness, everyone will know who did it because she'll be the only one upstairs," Mandie reasoned. "Come on. Let's go downstairs and get this over with."

Mandie led the way, and Celia made certain the door to their room was closed so that Snowball couldn't get out.

Most of the other girls in the school were already milling around downstairs. It was too cold to go outside, so everyone had to stay inside. Mandie and Celia found two seats in the parlor near the Christmas tree and sat there silently watching and listening as the other students buzzed around the room.

Soon there was the sound of rigs pulling up in front of the school and laughter and talking outside as the boys from Mr. Chadwick's School arrived.

All the girls became silent and quickly grabbed places to sit wherever they could find them. Mandie and Celia watched through the doorway for Tommy and Robert.

"Welcome to our school, Mr. Chadwick and all your young men," Miss Prudence announced at the front door. "We are glad to have you. Come into the parlor. I believe most of the young ladies are in there."

"Thank you for inviting us, Miss Heathwood." Mr. Chadwick returned the greeting amidst the murmured thanks from his students.

Mandie's heart beat faster.

Celia leaned over to her. "My hands are all wet," she whispered.

Tommy Patton and Robert Rogers were among the first to enter the parlor. Together, they spotted Mandie and Celia right away.

"Hello, Miss Amanda. How are you?" Tommy greeted Mandie with a smile. Then under his breath he added, "We have been admonished to mind our manners."

Mandie grinned mischievously, going along with him. "Fine, thank you," she said quite properly. "And how are you, Mr. Thomas?"

"Sorry, Miss Celia," Robert began, "but you heard Mr. Thomas. We have to keep this thing formal today per instructions from our headmaster, Mr. Chadwick. So I am supposed to ask how you are. And how are you, Miss Celia?"

Celia laughed nervously. "I am fine, Mr. Robert," she replied. "And I hope you are the same. Please have a seat."

"Yes, do," Mandie said. She and Celia moved closer together to give the boys room to sit on the long settee with them.

Their conversation continued on, stilted and unnatural, because Mr. Chadwick and Miss Prudence were keeping close watch on their students. Mandie and Tommy talked about Tommy's home in Charleston, South Carolina, which Mandie and her parents had visited. Mandie had seen the ocean for the first time then. Celia and

Robert joined in with a question or comment here and there, but the other two did most of the talking.

Millie, the dining room maid, and the extra maids hired for this get-together came in with tea trays and began serving.

Mandie accepted the dainty cup of hot tea and frowned. "I don't see why we can't have cocoa or something other than tea," she protested to her friends.

Celia laughed. "But then it wouldn't be afternoon tea," she said. "It would be afternoon hot cocoa."

They all laughed and the cups wobbled in the two girls' hands.

"I agree with Mandie," Robert said. "Not everyone likes hot tea."

"I suppose we're stuck with hot tea, though, until we grow up and can serve what we want in our own homes," Tommy remarked.

At that moment Celia screamed and spilled her tea. Teacups all around the room clattered, and other girls screamed. An uninvited visitor had startled everyone.

Snowball walked nonchalantly up to Mandie with a live mouse in his mouth and sat down.

"Snowball!" Mandie cried, lifting her feet. "Snowball, go away!"

"Get, Snowball!" Celia scolded the white kitten. "Get away from here!"

Snowball looked up at his mistress as if not understanding her reaction to his bringing her the treasure he had caught.

Mandie gave him a little shove with her toe. Snowball quickly let go of the mouse, and it ran under the Christmas tree. Snowball disappeared through the doorway.

All the other students hurried out of the parlor and gathered in the hallway.

"Let me see if I can find that mouse," Tommy volunteered. He stooped under the tree and shook various ornaments, hoping to scare the mouse from its hiding place. But nothing happened.

Miss Prudence walked up to Mandie. "How did that cat get out of your room?" she demanded. "I told you he would not be allowed anywhere else."

"I-I'm sorry, Miss Prudence," Mandie told her. "We were certain we shut the door when we left our room."

"Snowball was down here in the parlor last night, too," Celia said. "And I know we closed the door then. Evidently, somebody is letting him out."

"April Snow is the only one not present here," Miss Prudence said. "April Snow." She tapped her foot impatiently. "Let me check on her."

As Miss Prudence left the room, Mandie told the boys about April's escapades and the mouse in their room.

Tommy looked around under the tree again. "Do you think the mouse Snowball had came from your room?" he asked.

"We hope so," Mandie said, exchanging glances with Celia. "Then we won't have to worry about finding it in our room."

"Well, evidently he got away," Tommy said, rising to sit back down on the settee.

"That's a smart cat, Mandie," Robert said. "He knew right where you were."

"Well, he didn't have to bring that mouse with him," Mandie protested. She shivered at the thought of it.

"Young ladies," Miss Hope called over the confusion

in the hallway. "Please return to the parlor. The mouse is gone."

"You young men, too," Mr. Chadwick ordered.

Things finally settled down, but everyone kept looking around the floor for the mouse.

Miss Hope walked over to Mandie on the settee. "My sister has gone upstairs to check on April," she said. "We think she must have let your kitten out of your room. The door was open."

Mandie and Celia looked at each other.

"We definitely shut the door, Miss Hope," Mandie told her. "Snowball is a smart cat, and he knows a lot of other things, but he hasn't learned to open doors yet."

"Don't worry about it, Amanda. It wasn't your fault," Miss Hope replied as she left the room.

Mandie sighed. "Let's talk about something else," she said. "My mother says she has a big surprise waiting for me when I get home for Christmas, but I can't figure out what it is." She gave them all the details about Uncle Ned's visit and his message.

"I hope it's something wonderful," Tommy told her. "Are y'all having visitors for Christmas this year?"

"Well, yes," Mandie replied. "Dr. Woodard and his family will be there for Christmas, and then Celia and her mother are coming for New Year's. I wish you and your family could come."

"I do, too," Tommy said. "But maybe we can make it the next time your mother invites us. My parents did give me permission to visit with your family at your home some holiday weekend after Christmas."

"Oh, that's great!" Mandie exclaimed. "Miss Prudence never lets us know very far ahead when we're going to have a holiday, but I suppose you will have the same holidays at Mr. Chadwick's."

"I'll let you know," Tommy promised. He paused for a minute, looking straight into her blue eyes. "Mandie," he said, "will you be my partner for dinner at our school tomorrow night?"

"Of course," Mandie replied, smiling. "I'd love to."

Following Tommy's lead, Robert asked Celia to be his partner, and she agreed also.

After the boys left and the girls were free to go to their rooms until time for supper, Mandie and Celia hurried up the steps.

"Mandie, are you going to give Tommy a Christmas present tomorrow night?" Celia asked anxiously as they entered their room.

"I suppose it's expected," Mandie replied. She looked around. "Snowball is not here," she said with concern.

"What are you going to give him?" Celia wanted to know. "I don't have a thing to give Robert."

Mandie stopped to think. "I don't know," she said. "Maybe we'd better ask Miss Hope about presents."

"Yes, I think we'd better," Celia agreed.

The girls went back downstairs and found Miss Hope in her office.

"You girls don't have to give the young men gifts," Miss Hope explained, "but it's the normal practice. We must have neglected to mention that to you, I'm sorry. One thing I should tell you, however," Miss Hope emphasized, "is that my sister insists that the presents be something very inexpensive and simple."

"We don't have a thing to give Tommy and Robert," Mandie said.

"Well, let's see what we can come up with," Miss Hope said thoughtfully. "I know. I have some handkerchief linen. You girls have plenty of time tonight to make some handkerchiefs for them. How will that do?"

"Oh, thanks, Miss Hope," Mandie said.

"We appreciate it," Celia added.

"Wait here," Miss Hope said. She hurried into the rooms she occupied with her sister and immediately returned with a roll of white linen, some needles, thread, thimbles, and a pair of scissors. "If you just roll and whip the edges like this"—she demonstrated as she spoke—"it will be simple, and I think it will look nice."

"I've done that before," Mandie said. "It'll be easy."

"I know how to do that, too," Celia said.

"Then if you want to, you could embroider their initial in the corner," Miss Hope suggested. "Here's some embroidery thread."

Gratefully, the girls took the supplies and turned to leave the room.

"Oh, I almost forgot," Mandie said, turning back. "Snowball has disappeared, Miss Hope. He's not in our room."

"I'll ask Aunt Phoebe to look for him. He can't be far away," Miss Hope assured her.

Mandie and Celia returned to their room and hurriedly changed clothes, hanging up the fancy dresses and putting on gingham frocks that they normally wore around the school.

Finally, seated on the windowseat, the two girls began their work. They cut the material into four large squares, which would make two handkerchiefs each for Tommy and Robert.

"I wish we had thought about this earlier," Celia said, quickly stitching the edge of one piece of material.

"Everything got delayed because we had to be out of school during the flu epidemic," Mandie reminded her.

"All that time out of school was pretty interesting, though," Celia admitted. "Solving that mystery about the bells in the church steeple was fun—most of it—now that I can look back on it. I did get a little scared now and then, though."

"I don't think we could have figured that all out if we hadn't had time out from school," Mandie said.

"But now we have to make up all that lost time when we come back after the holidays," Celia reminded her. She accidentally pricked her finger with the needle. "Ouch!" she cried, quickly sucking her finger.

"Be careful," Mandie warned. "If your finger bleeds, you'll get it all over the handkerchief. You'd better run some cold water on it."

"I guess I'd better." Celia stood and laid her needlework on the windowseat. "Be right back."

Mandie continued her sewing as her friend left the room. Celia left the door partly open, and Mandie could hear her running water in the bathroom.

Suddenly Celia screamed. "Mandie! Mandie! Come quick!"

Mandie threw down her sewing and hurried across the hall to the bathroom. There was Celia standing on top of the lid to the commode. "What's the matter?" Mandie asked.

"There! Down there!" Celia cried, excitedly pointing to the floor. "A mouse ran under the bathtub!"

Mandie looked at the claw feet of the huge tub and stepped back, bending to look under it. "I don't see anything," she said.

"It was the same mouse Snowball had in the parlor," Celia moaned, still standing on top of the commode.

"How do you know it's the same one?" Mandie demanded. "Mice all look alike."

"I just know," Celia insisted.

"Come on," Mandie said, taking Celia's hand and helping her down. "Let's get out of here."

"I hope it doesn't come out and get in our room." Celia backed toward the door.

"Let's close the door real tight and go find Uncle Cal," Mandie suggested, closing the door behind them. "He can put a trap in there."

"Or maybe Aunt Phoebe has found Snowball, and he could catch it," Celia added.

The girls hurried downstairs to the kitchen where Aunt Phoebe was preparing supper. Uncle Cal was stoking the huge iron cookstove. At Uncle Cal's feet, Snowball was busy licking up a saucerful of milk.

"Snowball! You found him!" Mandie exclaimed.

At the sound of his mistress' voice the white kitten stopped long enough to look up at her and then continued eating.

"He come straight to de kitchen when y'all skeerd him out of de parlor," Aunt Phoebe told them. "He know a good place when he find one."

"Well, we know a better place for him, Aunt Phoebe," Mandie said. "Celia saw a mouse in our bathroom upstairs."

"It's the same one Snowball had in the parlor," Celia added.

Uncle Cal and Aunt Phoebe looked at each other and shook their heads.

"I sho' hopes it be de same one," Uncle Cal said. "Don't want dis house to git full of mice."

"We ain't never seed any mouses till dat one showed up in yo' room," Aunt Phoebe added.

"I'll set a trap in de bathroom," Uncle Cal told the girls as he headed for the pantry.

"He's under the bathtub," Celia explained.

"Jes' you girls be mighty careful how you walks 'round in dat bathroom now whilst de trap be dere," the old man said, coming out of the pantry with a mousetrap in his hand.

The girls watched as Aunt Phoebe sliced a tiny chip off a block of cheese sitting in a round wooden box on the sideboard nearby. Uncle Cal took it and set the trap, catching the spring with the latch on the piece of cheese.

"We's gotta put a stop to dese mouses runnin' round dis house," Aunt Phoebe fussed, "even if we has to put a stop to dat April gal comin' to dis school. Ain't never had dis trouble befo'."

Mandie carried Snowball as she and Celia followed Uncle Cal back upstairs to the bathroom. The two girls watched Uncle Cal set the trap under the tub.

"Be sho' dat cat don't git in heah," Uncle Cal cautioned. "He might git caught in dat trap."

"We'll see that he stays in our room, Uncle Cal," Mandie assured him.

The girls took Snowball back to their room and hurriedly went back to their sewing. But as they worked, they discussed plans for making sure that April didn't let Snowball out again.

When it was time for supper, the girls hid near the stairway and waited for April to leave her room, then followed her downstairs. And after supper was over, they rushed up the stairs ahead of her.

Snowball was still in their room, now curled up in the middle of the bed sound asleep.

"Well, I guess we outdid her this time," Mandie said triumphantly.

"But we've got all day tomorrow and tomorrow night to worry about before we go home the next morning." Celia sighed.

"I think we can manage," Mandie said. "Let's get these handkerchiefs done."

Chapter 3 / Visit to Mr. Chadwick's School

The next day, by staying alert and watching April Snow's every move without her knowledge, Mandie and Celia were able to keep Snowball in their room and April out of it.

Time dragged by with classes most of the day while the girls all wished the time away until they could go to the boys' school for dinner. The teachers had trouble holding their students' attention and reminded the girls of the examinations that were coming up after the Christmas holidays.

At last, with classes over for the day, the girls were free. Mandie and Celia breathed sighs of relief as they entered their room and closed the door. They had the rest of the afternoon to get dressed for dinner.

Mandie reached into the chifferobe and took out her red velvet dress while Celia chose her green one.

Mandie turned back to the bed and saw Snowball waking up. He sat up and washed his face with his paws. "Snowball, you have to get off the bed," Mandie told him, giving him a little shove and brushing off the bedspread.

"You're going to have white hairs all over the counter-pane, and they'll get on our dresses."

Reluctantly Snowball jumped down and sat on the rug.

The girls spread their dresses on the bed and rum-maged through the bureau drawers, looking for under-wear, stockings, and jewelry.

Mandie climbed onto a chair to reach the top of the chifferobe.

"What are you doing up there?" Celia asked.

Mandie pulled down two boxes and handed them to Celia. "We have to wear our good slippers with those dresses, don't you think?"

"Yes, I suppose so, but it's awfully cold outside to wear these flimsy things," Celia replied, taking her slippers from one of the boxes.

Mandie removed hers from the other box. "I know it's cold outside, but we're only going to be outside long enough to get to the boys' school, and that's not far away."

Celia sorted her jewelry on the bureau. "Do you know if April Snow is being allowed to go?" she asked.

"I heard Miss Prudence tell Miss Hope this morning that she would be allowed to go because it's Christmas-time," Mandie answered, laying out a fresh petticoat. "But she said that when school reopens after the holidays, April will still be restricted to her room except for meals and classes." Mandie paused for a moment. "In a way I'm glad she *is* going," she said slowly. "I'd hate for her to be left alone here in this big house while everyone else is having fun."

"But, Mandie, she brought it on herself," Celia re-minded her.

"I know, and I don't know why she does all these things," Mandie said with a sigh. "Anyhow, let's get dressed."

The two girls primped and preened before the mirror, and when they had everything adjusted to their satisfaction, they grabbed their neatly wrapped gifts for Tommy and Robert, shut Snowball in the room, and hurried downstairs to join the other students in the parlor.

A few moments later Miss Prudence entered the room, wearing her winter coat, gloves, scarf, and hat.

"Young ladies, we're ready to embark on our journey," the headmistress told the girls. "Please put on your coats and hats and line up in the hallway. Uncle Cal and Aunt Phoebe have our rigs in the driveway, and the rigs Mr. Chadwick sent are now approaching from the road."

The students quickly slipped into their winterwear and waited, chattering quietly among themselves.

Miss Prudence cleared her throat. "Young ladies," she addressed them again, "please be on your very best behavior tonight. Remember the school's reputation, and remember that we will be guests at Mr. Chadwick's school." Calling to Miss Hope at the front door, she said, "Sister, please open the door and let the girls start loading."

Mandie and Celia were among the first to leave, and they quickly took places in the rig Uncle Cal was driving.

"Oh, Mandie," Celia whispered, "I'm so nervous I won't be able to eat a thing."

"Me, too," Mandie admitted. Looking up, she saw April Snow taking a seat in the back of the rig, and she nudged Celia. "April is in this rig," she whispered.

Mandie saw Celia try to look behind them without turning her head, but she couldn't. And Miss Prudence was standing at the front with Uncle Cal, watching.

"I hope Snowball is still in our room," Celia said quietly. "April was downstairs before us, and I didn't see her leave the parlor after we came down, so I don't think she had a chance to let him out."

As soon as the last of the girls found places in Mr. Chadwick's rigs, Uncle Cal picked up the reins and drove off at Miss Prudence's command.

Mandie and Celia had never seen Mr. Chadwick's School for Boys. So when the rig drove up a long winding driveway through corridors of trees and came to a stop in front of something that looked like a giant castle, they were speechless. The huge gray stone structure was adorned with turrets, gables, balconies, and gargoyles.

"Whew!" Mandie exclaimed, alighting from the rig. "It's got everything but a moat."

"What a place!" Celia cried, joining her friend in the yard before the monstrosity. "Robert and Tommy live *here*?"

"I think I'd rather live in our school," Mandie said. "At least it's a real house and not a spooky thing like this."

"Young ladies," Miss Prudence called to the students as they stepped down from the rigs, "get in line quickly, please."

Mr. Chadwick stood in the huge double-door entranceway. He hurried down the stone steps to greet Miss Prudence. "Welcome to our school, Miss Heathwood and young ladies," he said, bending to take Miss Prudence's hand. "Please come in."

Miss Prudence beckoned to the girls, and they immediately fell into line behind her as she took Mr. Chadwick's arm and entered the huge building.

Mandie and Celia gasped again as they viewed the

entrance hallway. The floor was made of shining black-and-white marble. Suits of armor stood along the wall, some with swords and some with spears. Tapestries decorated the high walls above the marble wainscoting. Several huge chandeliers hung from overhead, and in the middle of each one was one of those new-fangled electric light bulbs. The original candlelights were not in use. Antique portraits, surrounded by velvet, silk, and tassels, hung along the way.

The girls jammed the hallway as Miss Prudence and Mr. Chadwick walked to the back where huge double doors stood open, revealing a banquet room large enough to hold five hundred people.

Long trestle tables were lined up through the room and were covered with white tablecloths, sparkling crystal, and shiny dishes and silverware. Holly and poinsettias decorated the room everywhere. Pieces of mistletoe hung from the huge chandeliers overhead. Comfortable chairs lined the walls.

All the girls gasped and sighed as they crowded in the doorway.

"If the young ladies will please find a seat, the young men will be in shortly," Mr. Chadwick announced. He turned to Miss Prudence. "Please excuse me," he said, leaving the room.

"Be seated, young ladies," Miss Prudence repeated as she and Miss Hope directed the students to places to sit.

Mandie sat down next to Celia and nudged her. "Did you ever see such a place? I had no idea!" Mandie whispered, looking around in awe.

"It's like stepping back into the seventeenth century," Celia replied.

As soon as the last girl was seated, uniformed maids came into the room and worked their way around, taking coats and hats as they were removed, and then leaving the room with the garments.

Miss Prudence stood at the doorway watching, and the girls dared not speak. Miss Hope walked to the back of the room and waited.

Mandie's heart beat wildly at the excitement of such a place. She had seen pictures of places like this in history books, but she didn't realize they were still in existence. *I can't wait to get home and tell Joe about this castle*, she thought. *He won't believe me.* Mandie's friend Joe always got involved in Mandie's adventures, but this was one he wouldn't be able to share.

Just then Mandie heard the sound of many feet in the hallway.

"Here they come!" Celia whispered very softly.

Mr. Chadwick led the boys into the room, and they stood quietly behind their headmaster, surveying their guests.

Mandie and Celia looked at the well-dressed young men. "I'm glad we got all dressed up," Mandie whispered. "Just look at them!"

"Young ladies, if you please," Mr. Chadwick began. "There are place cards on the tables. The young men know where their seats are, and they will come forward to lead you young ladies to the tables." Turning to the boys behind him, he said, "Now if you will each please step forward and claim your partner."

The boys moved around the room taking the girls one by one to the table assigned to them. There were already chairs around the tables, and the group stood behind these until the last ones had been claimed.

Tommy Patton and Robert Rogers were among the last to find their partners.

Mandie and Celia, still speechless, just smiled up at the two boys and accompanied them to the table.

After Mr. Chadwick returned thanks for the food, there was a loud shuffling noise as chairs were pulled out from the tables and everyone was seated. After they sat down, Mandie and Celia laid their gifts for the boys in their laps. Miss Prudence and Miss Hope sat on either side of Mr. Chadwick at the head table.

Finally the tension was broken, and the room was filled with laughter and conversation as the dinner began.

"How can you live in such a castle?" Mandie asked Tommy as the maids started bringing the food to the tables.

"I have to live here because my parents sent me here," Tommy said with a sigh. "You see, my father went to school here."

"Oh, I see," Mandie said. "So did my mother—I mean she went to my school, too." She turned to Robert. "And so did Celia's mother."

"My mother and Mandie's were friends," Celia added.

"Guess I'm the outsider," Robert said. "Nobody in my family ever went to this school."

"By the way, did Snowball ever catch that mouse?" Tommy asked.

Mandie and Celia brought the boys up-to-date.

"There's April Snow over at the next table," Mandie said, glancing in that direction.

April, dressed in the latest New York fashion, carried on a conversation with a tall handsome lad beside her.

"I wonder what she's telling that boy," Celia said. "She hardly ever talks to anyone."

"She really does look pretty," Mandie said.

At that moment a group of musicians came in, dressed in festive costumes, and carrying musical instruments. They sat down in a corner of the room, and began playing and singing Christmas carols. The buzz of conversation died down as the group sang.

Mr. Chadwick beckoned to the students to begin eating as the last of the savory food was placed on the tables.

Mandie finally felt herself relaxing in the pleasant atmosphere. Celia seemed to be at ease also.

Later, as they finished their meal, Mandie noticed various ones across the room exchanging Christmas presents, so she took her package from her lap and handed it to Tommy. "Merry Christmas, Tommy," she said, smiling as he also withdrew a tiny package from his pocket.

He handed it to her. "Merry Christmas, Mandie," he said, hastily unwrapping his gift from her. "Handkerchiefs! Exquisitely done! I needed these. Thanks for being a mind reader."

"You're welcome," Mandie said, pulling the paper off the present he had given her. She opened a small white box and cried, "A sand dollar on a chain! Oh, thank you, Tommy! I love it!" She held up the necklace for the others to see.

Celia showed Mandie the gift she had just unwrapped from Robert—a filmy white silk scarf. "Look! Isn't it beautiful?"

"Yes," Mandie agreed. "Did Robert like his handkerchiefs?"

Celia nodded enthusiastically.

After the maids removed the dinner plates and food, they brought in the dessert—tiny individual Christmas cakes, covered with red, green, and white icing.

As one of the maids placed a tiny cake in front of Mandie, she leaned over to Tommy and said, "This dinner must have cost your school a fortune."

Tommy laughed. "We pay enough tuition to cover this and more," he said.

Suddenly Celia tugged at Mandie's sleeve. "April Snow is gone!" she whispered.

Mandie turned quickly to stare at the empty chair where April had been sitting. Tommy and Robert followed her gaze.

"I wonder where she went," Mandie replied.

"There's one thing for sure," Tommy assured the girls. "It's too far for her to walk back to your school in this cold weather."

Celia tossed her auburn curls to look in Miss Prudence's direction. "I wonder if Miss Prudence knows she left."

The headmistress seemed completely absorbed in conversation with Mr. Chadwick. However, Miss Hope was looking at April's empty chair and frowning.

"Well, there's nothing we can do about it," Robert told the girls. "Maybe she'll come back in a little while."

"I doubt that," Mandie replied with a sigh.

As the evening passed, April didn't return to the dining room, and Mandie worried about what she might be doing. But Robert was right. There was nothing they could do about it.

As soon as everyone had finished dessert, Mr. Chadwick rose and addressed the students. "Young ladies, we will now have a skit put on by the young men who didn't have partners for this dinner. As you all probably know, we have one-third more students than Miss Heathwood.

That left a few of our students free to perform for us. I hope you enjoy it."

The musicians struck a chord, and a curtain covering the entire wall at one end of the room was slowly drawn back, revealing a lighted stage set with a scene for the holidays.

The students watched as the story of Jesus' birth unfolded in the drama on stage. Joseph and Mary were looking for a place to stay and were refused at the inn.

At first Mandie wondered where a boys' school found a girl to play Mary, but as she looked again, she couldn't tell if the actor was a boy or girl. Wearing loose robes and a hood over the head, the character of Mary spoke in low tones.

Mandie's ears perked up as she listened intently to the dialogue. Suddenly she turned to Celia. "I do believe that's April playing the part of Mary!" she whispered excitedly.

Celia nodded in agreement. Robert and Tommy understood and watched carefully to see if Mandie could be right.

Robert whispered, "I think it's Stan. He's about that size."

"Yes, that's Stan," Tommy agreed.

Mandie and Celia looked at each other.

"Are you sure?" Mandie asked.

"To be honest, no," Tommy admitted.

The scene continued on, but even when the curtain closed, they still weren't certain who was playing the part of Mary. After a lot of applause, the curtain opened again for a bow. The actors lined up in a row across the stage with "Mary" in the middle. As that person bowed, the hood fell away, revealing none other than April Snow.

Mandie gasped. "I thought so!" she exclaimed. "It is April!"

"How did she get into that play?" Celia wondered aloud.

"Well, I wonder what happened to Stan?" Tommy looked puzzled. "I heard he was going to play that character since we don't have any girls at our school."

Mandie glanced across the room to Miss Prudence. She looked shocked, while Miss Hope was smiling in wonderment.

"I don't think I'd want to be in April's shoes when we get back to our school," Mandie commented.

After a final bow from the cast, the curtain closed, and the applause died away.

Mr. Chadwick got quickly to his feet and tapped a fork on his glass for attention. "Young ladies," he began, "we are very honored that one of your group could participate in our play. A young lady playing a woman is certainly better than having one of our boys do so, and we thank you." He fidgeted with his lapel. "This was, however, a complete surprise to me and evidently to your headmistress. I am sure it will be interesting to learn how it all came about. We thank you for coming tonight. It was indeed an honor to have all of you visit us. We wish you all a merry Christmas and a happy New Year. We will see you next year."

After another round of applause, the group broke up as Miss Hope and Miss Prudence rounded up their students for the journey back to their own school.

When the maids brought the girls' wraps back into the room, Tommy helped Mandie into her coat.

Mandie smiled up at him. "Thanks for the sand dollar, Tommy," she said. "I'll wear it for Christmas Day."

"And I thank you for the beautiful handkerchiefs," Tommy replied. "I'll see you after the holidays."

The girls piled into the waiting rigs and returned to their school. Holiday spirit filled the air.

Back at school, as the girls unloaded, Mandie and Celia watched for April Snow. But she was not in any of the rigs. Neither was Miss Prudence.

All the girls wanted to linger downstairs to see what happened when Miss Prudence and April returned. But Miss Hope gently urged them upstairs to their rooms.

"I'm sure you young ladies are all tired," she said. "But don't forget, you must get busy packing if you haven't already done so because you may leave just as soon as someone comes for you in the morning. So I would strongly urge you to go upstairs and prepare for your journey home tomorrow."

That was all the girls needed. They quickly hurried upstairs to their rooms.

"Amanda," Miss Hope called to Mandie when she was halfway up the first flight of stairs. "I'm sorry, dear, I almost forgot to tell you. Your grandmother sent word here while we were gone. Uncle Cal says she and Hilda will pick you up in the morning in time to catch the train for home."

Mandie grinned. "Thanks, Miss Hope. I'll be ready."

Celia smiled when she heard the news. "Hilda must really be feeling better if she's well enough to travel," she said.

They continued up the stairs to their room. "Yes, thank the Lord," Mandie replied. "So Mother and Uncle John won't be coming after me." She shrugged. "Oh, well, I'm glad Hilda is better, and I'm glad Grandmother is going home with me."

When they reached their room Mandie opened the

door. Snowball was curled up asleep in the middle of the bed again, and he opened one eye to look at his mistress.

Mandie laughed. "Snowball, you lazy thing," she said, stroking his soft white fur. "You should be catching that mouse instead of sleeping all the time when we go out."

"That mouse must not be in our room any longer," Celia reasoned. "Otherwise Snowball would have found it by now."

"Don't worry. If it's gone, April will just find another one to put in here while we've gone home," Mandie said. "That is, unless Miss Prudence expels her or something for being in that play tonight."

"I imagine there will be some pretty bad punishment," Celia agreed.

"Well, let's get packing," Mandie said, throwing off her hat and gloves. "Just think. This time tomorrow I'll be home, and I'll know what that big surprise is that my mother has for me."

Chapter 4 / Home for Christmas

Celia and Mandie waited with their luggage downstairs in the alcove near the front door. They were excitedly talking about the upcoming holidays.

Mandie held Snowball on her lap and peered through the front window. She sighed. "I wish Grandmother would hurry and get here," she said. "I want to go home and see what Mother's surprise is."

"She'll be here in time for you to get the train. You can't leave any sooner than the train leaves anyhow," Celia replied. "But I know how you feel. I'll be glad to see Aunt Rebecca and to get home to my mother."

Mandie stood up. "Well, here comes your Aunt Rebecca with Uncle Cal now," she said, noticing an approaching carriage. "And behind her is Ben, driving Grandmother's rig."

The two girls ran to the front door. Mandie held Snowball in one hand and threw the door open with the other as Celia's Aunt Rebecca Hamilton hurried up the steps.

"I do hope you are ready, Celia, so we can catch the train going back to Richmond," the tiny, dark-haired lady said as she stepped into the hallway out of the cold.

"Yes, ma'am, I'm ready," Celia said, indicating her nearby luggage. "Is Uncle Cal going to take us to the station?"

Mandie held the front door open a little ways and called to her grandmother's driver as he halted the rig behind Uncle Cal's. "Ben!" she shouted. "Where's Grandmother? And Hilda?"

Ben grinned as he stepped down from the rig and patted the horse's head. "Miz Taft, she say you git in dis rig, and I goes back to fetch her and dat Hilda girl."

"All right," Mandie said. She turned to Aunt Rebecca. "There's no use in Uncle Cal going to the station," she said as Ben came into the front hallway. "We can all ride in Grandmother's rig."

"But, dear, will we make the train on time?" Aunt Rebecca asked. "You know our train leaves about thirty minutes before yours."

Ben spoke up. "Miz Taft, she sittin' ready to go," he said. "I already got her luggage in de rig. She say she jes' don't want dat Hilda girl to come to dis school 'cause she might run away and come heah sometime agin." He picked up Mandie's luggage.

"All right then, we'll go with you," Aunt Rebecca replied.

"My luggage is over here, Ben," Celia told the Negro driver.

Ben was right. When they pulled into the long driveway of Mrs. Taft's huge mansion, the door opened, and Mrs. Taft and Hilda stepped outside.

"Why, Rebecca Hamilton!" Grandmother Taft exclaimed in surprise. "How are you? It has been a long time." She helped Hilda into the rig and then accepted Ben's assistance into the carriage herself.

Celia's aunt moved over on the seat to give Mrs. Taft room. "It certainly has," she replied. "I don't believe I've seen you since I was a student at the Heathwood School with your daughter, Elizabeth, and with Celia's mother."

"Hello, Hilda," Mandie greeted the thin brown-haired girl who came to sit between her and Celia in the rig. "I'm so glad to see you." She stroked Snowball's white fur as she spoke.

Hilda smiled at Mandie and then at Celia. Even though she had never uttered more than a few words since Mandie and Celia found her hiding in the attic of the school, Hilda showed her love for the two girls in her facial expressions. She obviously realized they were her friends.

Mandie took Hilda's gloved hand in hers. "I'm so glad you got well, Hilda," she said. "When you ran away in all that snow and hid in the church, you got so sick, and I was real worried about you. I prayed for God to make you well and He did."

Hilda smiled at Mandie again. "God. Well," she said simply.

Celia and Mandie both laughed.

"It makes us so happy when you understand what we say, Hilda," Celia told her, "because we love you."

"Love." Hilda smiled.

Mrs. Taft and Rebecca Hamilton talked all the way to the station and continued talking in the waiting room at the depot.

Mandie and Celia tried to keep a conversation going with Hilda as the three girls and Snowball sat on a bench near the adults. Sometimes Hilda seemed to understand what they said, but sometimes she didn't.

"She's so much better than she was when we found her," Mandie remarked.

"And it's so wonderful that she keeps getting better," Celia replied.

A train whistle sounded in the distance and kept blowing as it neared the depot. Ben picked up Celia's luggage and walked out onto the platform.

Aunt Rebecca came over to Celia. "Time to say goodbye," she prompted.

Mandie looked up at the tiny lady. "Miss . . . Aunt Rebecca, can't you come to our house for New Year's Eve, too, when Celia and her mother come?" she asked.

"Thank you for asking, dear," Aunt Rebecca replied. "But I have made other plans." She took Celia's hand and led her out to the platform.

Mandie picked up Snowball, and she and Mrs. Taft followed them out. "Don't forget," Mandie called to her friend as Celia and her aunt boarded the waiting train, "You and your mother promised to come for New Year's."

Mrs. Taft stepped up behind Mandie, rested her hand on her granddaughter's shoulder, and called to Celia. "Tell your mother I look forward to seeing her," she said with a smile. "It has been many years."

With a stream of "Merry Christmas" shouts, Celia and Aunt Rebecca were on their way. And soon Grandmother Taft, Hilda, Mandie, and Snowball boarded their train for Franklin.

Jason Bond, the caretaker for Mandie's Uncle John, met them at the depot.

"Mother didn't come, Mr. Jason?" Mandie questioned him as he piled the luggage in the rig.

Jason Bond helped Hilda and Mrs. Taft into the carriage. "No, Missy," he said. "Your mother and your Uncle John had to go over to Tellico early this morning. Mr. Wright, a good friend of theirs, is awfully sick."

Mandie took a seat next to Hilda and settled Snowball in her lap. "When will they be back?"

"Don't rightly know," Jason Bond replied as he climbed into the driver's seat. "They said they'd be back as soon as Mr. Wright shows some improvement." He shook the reins, and the rig moved forward.

"Aw, shucks!" Mandie sighed loudly.

"Amanda!" Mrs. Taft reprimanded her. "The man is sick, and your mother and John are trying to help out."

"I'm sorry, Grandmother," Mandie said. "I'm just so eager to find out what Mother's big surprise for me is."

"It will just have to keep until your mother returns home," her grandmother said.

"Yes, ma'am," Mandie said meekly. "Where is Tellico, Mr. Jason? How far is it?"

"It's a purty fur piece over the mountain and down the other side," Mr. Bond told her. "Looks like a good snow might be coming. If it does, it'll take them a good while to get home."

Mandie sighed again. *So, I still don't know what the surprise is*, she thought. *Oh, why did my mother pick this day to go off? Why couldn't she wait till I got home?*

"Your friend Joe Woodard is at the house," Mr. Bond told her. "He came with his mother and father yesterday. Dr. and Mrs. Woodard left Joe at the house while they went with your parents to care for Mr. Wright."

Mandie bristled at the term *your parents*. "Mr. Bond, you know that Uncle John is not my parent." She hoped that using his last name indicated a formal tone and set him straight. "I have only one *parent*. My father is . . . no longer living, and my mother married Uncle John, my father's brother. So I have a mother and a stepfather, not two *parents*."

"Yes, yes, Missy. I'm sorry. I know John Shaw isn't your father."

"Then please remember that," Mandie said in a trembling voice. "No one could ever replace my father." Mandie felt badly about the way the words came out, and she expected her grandmother to scold her, but Mrs. Taft said nothing.

Mr. Bond reached back and patted Mandie's hand.

"At least I'm glad Joe is at the house," Mandie said, trying to smile as she fought back tears. She looked down at her white kitten. "Wake up, Snowball, you lazy cat."

Snowball had slept during the whole train ride, and when they got in the rig, he immediately went back to sleep in her lap. But now, at the commanding tone of his mistress's voice, he blinked his blue eyes and began unfolding from his sleeping position.

Mandie picked him up and looked into his sleepy eyes. "I'll be glad to get you home and let you loose, Snowball," she said. "I know you're tired of being shut up."

Hilda suddenly leaned forward and smoothed the kitten's fur. "Snowball," she said.

Mandie handed her the kitten, and Hilda immediately cuddled him in her arms. As Snowball began to purr, Hilda started humming.

"I think this trip will be good for Hilda," Mrs. Taft said. "She has been shut up too much lately, too, what with being sick and all. I hope you and Joe will include her in whatever you do for the holidays, Amanda. I'm not sure she's happy with me. Maybe I shouldn't have taken her into my home. Maybe I should have placed her in a home where there are other young people."

Hilda didn't seem to be listening, but suddenly she

reached forward and grabbed Mrs. Taft's hand. "No!" she said loudly.

"I love you, dear," Grandmother Taft told her. "I just want you to be happy."

"Happy. Love," Hilda repeated the words with a smile.

"Well, I guess that settles that," Mandie commented.

Moments later the rig pulled up in front of John Shaw's huge white house and came to a halt at the hitching post.

"Here we are," Mr. Bond announced.

Mandie surveyed the grounds. The grass and flowers behind the picket fence were dead now. The summer-house at the side looked cold and uninviting against the gray winter sky. The big tree limbs in front were bare as they reached up toward the third story of the house. The rocking chairs that occupied the long front porch in the summer had been put away. Only the porch swing remained, swaying and creaking on its chains.

Mandie took Snowball from Hilda and then quickly jumped from the rig, running up the long walkway toward the house. The front door opened and Joe hurried out to meet her.

Joe Woodard, Mandie's lifelong friend, was a tall, gangly lad with unruly brown hair, brown eyes, and a determined chin.

"Oh, Joe, I'm so glad you're here since nobody else is," Mandie exclaimed, meeting him halfway.

"Now that's a nice welcome," Joe teased with a solemn face. "You're glad I'm here because no one else is."

"Oh, Joe, I didn't mean it like it sounded," Mandie protested. "I'm always glad to see you. I don't know what I'd do without your friendship."

"I'll remember that a few years from now," Joe replied

as they turned to walk toward the house.

Mandie looked puzzled.

"A few years from now when we get old enough for me to ask you to marry me," he explained with a mischievous grin.

"Please don't ruin everything by talking like that," Mandie fussed as he opened the door for her.

Joe didn't have time for an answer because Mrs. Taft, Hilda, and Mr. Bond caught up with them. And the whole household waited in the entrance hall to welcome Mandie home.

Aunt Lou, the tall, buxom housekeeper, quickly embraced Mandie. "I's glad you's home, my chile," she said enthusiastically.

Mandie squeezed her tight. "I'm glad to see you all, too, Aunt Lou"—she looked around—"and Liza . . . and Jenny . . . and why, there's Abraham, too!"

The servants all smiled and greeted Mandie while Snowball stayed close, rubbing against her legs.

Aunt Lou turned to Liza. "Now you goes upstairs wid my chile and help her change into sumpin' more like we wears heah, Liza," she ordered. Then she grinned at Mandie. "Git rid of dem fancy clothes whilst you heah, my chile."

Liza followed Mandie upstairs to her room while Aunt Lou got Hilda settled in a room next to Mandie and across the hall from Mrs. Taft's room. Snowball was allowed to roam the house.

As soon as Liza closed the door to Mandie's room, Mandie grabbed the servant girl's hand. "Liza, what is the big surprise my mother has for me?" she asked.

Liza looked at her, plainly puzzled. "Big surprise? I don't be knowin' of no big surprise."

"Oh, Liza, please tell me," Mandie begged. "I won't let anyone know you told me. Please?"

"Now you listens hear, Missy 'Manda. I don't be knowin' what you's talkin' 'bout," Liza said firmly.

Mandie sighed. "Oh, shucks!"

Then Liza began dancing around the room, laughing. "But I knows who does know. Dat I does."

"Who knows, Liza? Who?" Mandie asked quickly.

Liza came to a halt in front of Mandie. "You promise you ain't gwine to repeat nuthin' I says, ain't you now?" she asked.

"Yes, I promise, Liza. Please hurry up and tell me."

"Well, I thinks it be like dis," Liza began as she moved about the room. "Early dis mawnin' I hears Miz 'Lizbeth whisperin' to Miz Doctor Lady when de messenger brang de word 'bout Mistuh Wright bein' 'bout to leave dis world. He be right sick, you knows."

"Please hurry, Liza. Tell me," Mandie begged, stomping her foot.

"Well, dat's all I knows." Liza walked over to the fireplace and stirred up the fire. "When dey sees me standin' right there by de sideboard where dey's gittin' coffee, dey shuts right up."

"You couldn't hear anything they said?"

"Didn't hear nuthin' dey say 'cause dey talk too low-like," Liza replied. "Now, I's s'posed to he'p you unpack, and den I's gwine downstairs to he'p git dinnuh on de table."

"Go ahead, Liza. I can do this myself." Mandie turned to the luggage Mr. Bond had deposited in her room. "Would you check on Hilda, too, in case Aunt Lou went back downstairs to work. We don't want Hilda running off somewhere again."

Liza started for the door. "I find dat Hilda girl, and I takes huh downstairs wid me," she promised.

Mandie pulled a gingham pinafore from her trunk.

"You better put on sumpin' warmer den dat 'cause it be gwine to snow," Liza said as she went out the door.

As Mandie pulled things out of the trunk, she piled them on her blue taffeta bedspread until she finally found the red plaid wool dress she had been looking for. She put it on. Then she sat on a stool in front of the blazing fire in the fireplace and changed her high-top boots to lower ones, all the while wondering what her mother's surprise was.

I know, she thought, *I'll ask Aunt Lou. She knows everything that goes on around here.*

As soon as she straightened up the mess in her room, she quickly ran downstairs in search of Aunt Lou. She found her by the linen closet, folding freshly washed sheets and putting them away.

"Aunt Lou, you always know everything," Mandie began, watching the woman work. She picked up a pillowcase and folded it herself.

"No, my chile, I don't knows ev'rythin', never," the Negro housekeeper said, smiling at her in that way that made Mandie feel special.

"I need to know something, and you probably know it," Mandie said, folding another pillowcase.

"Whatever my chile need, I finds out," Aunt Lou replied.

"I want to know what the big surprise is that my mother has for me," Mandie said quickly, watching the old woman's face.

Aunt Lou gave her a sly glance and went right on folding sheets. "I thought you say you *needs* to know somethin', but heah you say you *wants* to know somethin'. Big diff'rence." She put her hands on her broad hips and looked sternly at Mandie.

"So you do know what I'm talking about," Mandie reasoned. "Please tell me what it is, Aunt Lou. Please?"

"I ain't tellin' you nuthin', my chile," Aunt Lou said. "Might as well give up. Wouldn't be right fo' me to ruin yo' mother's su'prise fo' you. No, it wouldn't."

Mandie stood there thinking for a moment. She was sure the old housekeeper knew what the secret was, and she knew Aunt Lou would never tell.

"Bettuh git in dat parlor and find dat doctuh boyfriend o' yours," Aunt Lou said, again folding sheets. "He be lonesome."

"All right," Mandie said, disappointed. And she went to look for Joe.

She found him lying in front of the huge fireplace in the parlor, staring at a checkerboard in front of him.

"I don't see any partner," Mandie teased. "Who is playing checkers with you?" She dropped down on the rug beside him.

"I'm waiting for you," Joe replied. "You take the red ones to match that red dress you've got on."

Mandie looked down at her dress and smiled. "You like my new dress?"

"I suppose it's all right. Must be new. Never saw it before." Joe handed her the stack of red checkers. "Come on. I'll beat you."

"I will beat you," Mandie laughed as they began the game.

But Mandie's mind was not on the game of checkers. She would wait until Joe was clearly winning before she asked her question.

At last her opening came.

"I'm ahead!" Joe announced, proudly surveying the board. "Better hurry if you're going to beat me."

Mandie sat back on her heels and looked Joe in the eye. "I'm more interested in asking you a question than I am in winning our game," she said. "Joe, do you know what the big surprise is that my mother has for me?"

"Just like a conniving woman," Joe said, mimicking his father. "Try to get a man in a good mood and then take advantage of it." He laughed.

"I am not a conniving woman," Mandie retorted. "I only want a simple answer to a simple question."

"Which I am not going to give to you," Joe said smugly. "Your turn."

"You can at least tell me whether you know what the secret is, please?" Mandie begged. She looked down at the board and shoved a checker forward.

"Why should I tell you and make your mother mad at me?" Joe asked, taking his turn.

"Because she's not here to tell me, and I just can't wait any longer," Mandie insisted. "I want to know."

"You'll have to wait until your mother gets back," he said.

"Joe, I thought you were my friend," Mandie pouted.

Joe looked straight into her blue eyes. "Believe me, Mandie. I am your friend. That's why I'm not going to tell you what the surprise is."

"Then you do know. Why won't you tell me?"

Joe jumped up, knocking the checkerboard and messing up the game. "Because knowing you, you're going to be madder than an old wet hen," he said. "You're not going to like it at all when you find out what the surprise is."

Mandie jumped up from the floor. "I'm not going to like the surprise?" she said in shock. "But all the time I thought it was going to be something nice. How do you know I won't like the surprise?"

"That's all I'm going to say." Joe strode over to a nearby armchair and sat down. "The subject is closed."

"Joe Woodard, I could . . . could . . ." Mandie was at a loss for words.

Suddenly Jason Bond came into the room, breaking the tension. "Looks like snow out there any minute now," he said. "Being Mr. and Mrs. Shaw aren't here, I think *we'd* better see about getting a Christmas tree in before it starts."

Joe and Mandie glanced out the window at the haze of snow clouds.

"Could we go find one as soon as we eat dinner, Mr. Jason?" Mandie asked.

"That's what I was going to suggest," Mr. Bond replied.

Just then Liza appeared in the doorway and said, "Aunt Lou, she say ev'rybody git to de dinin' room fast. Dinner be on de table. Quick now!"

"We're coming," Mandie said. She turned to Joe. "We'd better hurry if we're going to get a tree."

Joe didn't move. "I'm not going with you to find a tree unless you promise not to mention a word about that stupid surprise," he said.

Mr. Bond looked at Joe, then at Mandie.

Mandie finally spoke. "All right, I promise. What else can I do?"

Joe grinned at Jason Bond. "Let's go eat, Mr. Jason," he said. "I think I know a good place to find a tree."

Mandie followed them into the dining room as her

thoughts raced. She had tried every way she knew to find out what her mother had in store for her, but she still didn't know what it was. Joe had said she wouldn't like it. *What on earth could Mother have to tell me that I won't like?* she wondered.

Mandie wished her mother would hurry home.

Chapter 5 / It Snowed and Snowed!

Everyone hurried through dinner, knowing the snowstorm would hit soon.

Mrs. Taft excused Mandie and Joe while she finished her coffee. "You may go now, but get your coats and wait for Mr. Bond in the hallway," she said.

When Mandie and Joe got up from the table, Hilda started to follow.

"No, Hilda, you stay here with me," Mrs. Taft said, grabbing the girl's hand.

"We could take her with us," Mandie offered.

"No, she runs away too often," Grandmother Taft replied. "And with a storm coming, I don't want her to get lost." She patted Hilda's hand. "You stay with me. We'll have some chocolate pie."

Hilda smiled at Mrs. Taft and sat back down as Joe and Mandie left the room.

"Guess I'd better hurry," Mandie said, rushing up the steps to get her coat and hat.

"Me, too," Joe said. Taking the steps two at a time, he walked briskly to the room he was occupying down the hall from Mandie's. Just as Mandie was about to enter her room, he stuck his head back out the door. "And don't bring that white cat," he said.

Mandie sighed angrily. "I'm not going to bring Snowball. You don't have to worry about that."

"Good," Joe said. "He's always running off somewhere, and we don't have time to hunt him."

"I said all right." Mandie stomped into her room and shut the door. *Why does Joe always have to be so bossy?* she thought to herself. She had better sense than to take Snowball out in the woods in this cold weather with snow fixing to fall. *Oh, I wish Uncle Ned would come. He could help us find a good Christmas tree. But I suppose he's at home in Deep Creek with other things to do.* Uncle Ned was an old Cherokee friend of her father's. When Jim Shaw died he had promised to watch over Mandie. He kept his promise. The Indian was old but he was still strong, active and alert.

Joe tapped on her door. "I'm ready," he called.

Mandie grabbed her heavy winter coat and hat, snatched up a scarf and a pair of wool gloves and hurried downstairs.

Mr. Bond met them in the hallway, dressed for the outdoors and carrying an axe. "Abraham has the wagon hitched up outside," he said. "I'd suggest going out to Mr. Shaw's land near the boardinghouse to look for a tree."

"You mean where Dr. Plumbley used to live?" Mandie replied. "That's a good idea."

As the wagon neared the woods where Mandie and her friends had searched for hidden treasure the last time Mandie was home, Mr. Bond slowed the horse. He turned to Mandie and Joe. "Suppose we leave the wagon here and walk through the trees there and see what we can find," he said.

"Fine," Mandie agreed.

"This is the very place I had in mind," Joe said, helping Mandie from the wagon.

As they tramped through the cold woods, they saw lots of small evergreens that would have made fine Christmas trees, but Mandie was determined to find a tree tall enough to touch the twelve-foot ceiling in the house.

"After all," she said, "this is my very first Christmas with my mother, and I want it to be special."

After walking along for some time in silence, Joe pointed ahead and cried, "Hey, how about that one?"

"Just what we need!" Mandie exclaimed, hurrying with the others toward it.

Mr. Bond took his axe and began swinging at the trunk of the tree. "Stand back now," he warned.

Mandie and Joe moved away from him. Every time Mr. Bond hit a lick at the tree there seemed to be an echo. At first Mandie didn't pay much attention to it. But then Mr. Bond missed a lick, and they still heard it.

Mandie looked at Joe. "Does it sound to you like someone else is chopping down a tree or something?"

Joe nodded. "I've been listening. I think there's someone else around here doing something."

Mr. Bond looked up. "Probably somebody after a Christmas tree," he said.

"But this is my Uncle John's land," Mandie protested.

"He never bothers about other people coming in here and getting a tree now and then," Mr. Bond said, resuming his chopping.

The echo sounded again. Then suddenly there was a loud crash nearby. Mandie and Joe looked at each other and ran off in the direction of the crash. Mr. Bond followed.

As they hurried through the trees, Mandie caught a glimpse of something moving. "What's that?" she cried.

"Stop or we'll shoot!" Joe yelled, even though none of them had a gun.

The noise stopped.

As the young people broke through the trees, they came face-to-face with a man and woman all bundled up with heavy coats, hats, and scarves. They were pulling at a small, freshly cut tree.

"Who are you?" Joe demanded.

"Don't shoot!" the man cried.

And as he spoke, Mandie recognized them. It was Jake and Ludie Burns, who lived in a tenant house on John Shaw's property.

The woman squinted at the young people. "Well, if'n it ain't John Shaw's niece!" she exclaimed.

"Oh, I'm glad to see you, Mrs. and Mr. Burns," Mandie said, rushing forward to embrace the old woman.

Joe shook hands with Mr. Burns. "Imagine finding you here," he said.

Mr. Bond greeted the couple, then said, "I told these young people that Mr. Shaw allowed other people to get Christmas trees off his property now and then—"

"We got permission yestiddy to cut a tree," Jake Burns explained.

"You'ns will hafta come see our house whilst you're home fer Christmas," Ludie Burns said. "We's got it all fixed up airtight and real purty, if I do say so."

"We'll come see it," Mandie promised. "Do you have any decorations for your tree?"

"We been amakin' some li'l doo-dads that oughta be 'nuff to make it look purty," Mrs. Burns replied.

"We'll bring you some things from Uncle John's attic," Mandie offered. "I know he has lots and lots of Christmas decorations up there. Remember when we got the furniture out of there for y'all's house? Well, we found all kinds of things up there then."

Joe laughed. "I'd say. There must be fifty years' worth of decorations up there."

Mr. Bond looked up at the sky through the bare trees. "I'm sure I felt a snowflake," he said. "We'd better be getting that tree cut."

Mandie looked all around and then at the Burnses. "How did you get here?" she asked.

"Oh, we got a wagon now, thanks to your uncle," Mr. Burns said. "It's back there on that side road." He indicated another side of the woods.

Mandie followed Joe and Mr. Bond as they started back toward the tree they were cutting. "We'll come see you tomorrow with the decorations," she called back to the old couple.

Mr. Bond stopped and turned around. "I don't know about that," he said. "If that storm is as bad as I expect, you won't be able to get that far."

"Why don't y'all just come on by the house now, and we'll give you some decorations?" Mandie said.

The old people agreed.

With Joe's help, Mr. Bond finished cutting down the tree and put it in the wagon. By that time the snow was falling fast and thick.

"Looks like you were right about the snow, Mr. Jason." Mandie sighed. "I hope my mother and Uncle John get back all right."

As they loaded the tree into the wagon, Jason Bond looked at the sky. "I doubt that they'll be coming home tonight," he said. "The snow is coming from that direction over there, and that's where they've gone."

Mandie groaned. After hopping into the wagon, she wrapped her scarf around her face, leaving only enough room to see out. The snow was icy, and she felt as if her face was freezing.

When they got back to the house, they found the place in a turmoil. Both Hilda and Snowball were missing! Mrs. Taft had thought that Hilda was asleep. The girl had lain down on her bed for a nap, and when Mrs. Taft checked on her, she seemed to be fast asleep.

No one had seen Snowball in quite a while, either. Liza had fed him in the kitchen and left him there after the dinner was cleared away.

Mrs. Taft paced up and down in the entrance hallway. "I just don't know what to do about that girl," she said. "If she went outdoors she didn't put on her coat. The blanket from her bed is missing, though. I keep thinking she will get over all this running-away business, but I just don't know."

Mr. Bond took charge. "Has the house been searched?" he asked.

"No, not all over," Mrs. Taft replied. "We mostly opened doors to the rooms and glanced inside. We just missed her a few minutes ago. And then Liza said she couldn't find Snowball, either."

Mandie removed her coat and hung it on the hall tree. "Hilda probably took Snowball with her wherever she went."

Joe and Mr. Bond hung their coats on the hall tree as well.

"Why don't we work our way upstairs all the way to the attic and then down again if necessary," Mandie suggested.

Just then Liza came into the hallway, and Joe immediately enlisted her help.

"Want me to get Aunt Lou, too?" Liza asked.

Mrs. Taft spoke up. "No, that won't be necessary," she said. "She's like I am—a little too old to go running up and down three flights of steps."

Again Mr. Bond took charge. "We should look in every room, behind all the doors, under the beds and any other place large enough to hide under," he told the young people.

Mandie knew this would be no small task. The three-story house also had an attic that would need to be checked. Each floor had a center hallway plus a cross hallway, and so many rooms that Mandie didn't even know how many there were.

The search party began in the parlor and then split up, with Mandie and Liza going one direction, while Joe and Mr. Bond went another.

Many of the rooms had not been occupied in years. As the doors were opened, the hinges creaked, and a musty odor filled the air.

In one of the rooms, Mandie batted at a large cobweb in disgust. "What this house needs is a good cleaning," she told Liza.

"Mr. Shaw say don't bother de rooms that ain't used 'cept when extra comp'ny comes," Liza defended herself. "And it take whole lot of comp'ny to fill up dis house, maybe a hunnerd people."

"I suppose so," Mandie said, looking under a high four-poster bed in an unoccupied room. "It'd take twenty maids to keep this place clean all the time. I don't see why my great-grandfather built such a big house."

"But Aunt Lou say dere used to be lots of Shaws,"

Liza replied. "Now de only Shaw living is Mr. John Shaw, 'cept you. And when you git married to dat doctuh boy, your name won't be Shaw no more."

Mandie blushed in spite of herself and turned to pull the door shut as she and Liza left the room. "Liza, you know I'm nowhere near old enough to talk about getting married," Mandie said. "Now keep your mind on what we're doing."

Liza grinned. "When de time come, you gwine to marry dat doctor boy. Jes' you wait and see."

Mandie led the way to the next room. "You must think you're a fortuneteller or something," she grumbled. "Come on. We've got to hurry and find Hilda and Snowball. If we can't find them in here, we'll have to look outside. And if they're out there, they might freeze to death. Every second counts."

Joe and Mr. Bond arrived at the stairs to the attic just before the girls. Walking ahead, they opened the attic door. Mandie and Liza were right behind them. Suddenly something white and furry swept past their legs from inside the attic. Everyone was startled.

Mandie whirled around. "Snowball!" she exclaimed. There at the bottom of the steps stood the white kitten, looking at them. Mandie turned back to the others. "Hilda must have brought him up here," she said. "Maybe she's here, too."

As they entered the attic, Mandie squinted in the dim light. The small windows gave little light since it was snowing outside.

"I'll get the lamp from the hall table downstairs," Joe volunteered. He ran down to get it and quickly returned.

Mr. Bond took a box of matches from his pocket and lit the lamp. As he held the lamp high, the others followed him around the attic between discarded furniture, old trunks, boxes, and odds and ends that had accumulated over the years.

"Nobody here," Jason Bond announced as they arrived back at the doorway.

Joe scratched his head. "But how did Snowball get in here?" he asked. "Liza, do you know if anybody has been up here today for any reason?"

"No, no, no!" Liza exclaimed. "Ain't nobody ever come up heah. Too spooky."

Mr. Bond headed downstairs. "I suppose Hilda has gone outside," he said, "so we might as well get our coats back on."

Blowing out the lamp, he set it on the table where it belonged. Mandie picked up Snowball, and they all made their way back to the front hallway.

Aunt Lou stood at the front door, holding it open for Jake and Ludie Burns, who had just arrived. They stomped their feet on the front porch, then stepped inside. When they heard about Hilda's disappearance, they offered to join the others in a search outside.

Spreading out in different directions, they all searched every place anyone could possibly hide. But as time went on, they became more and more worried. The snow was getting heavier, the sky was getting darker, and the temperature was getting colder.

Joe, Mandie, and Liza had just finished searching the barns on their way back from the fields when Abraham, the gardener, hurried out to them. "Come on back!" he called. "Come on back!"

They hurried to catch up with him as he continued on to tell Mr. Bond and the Burnses to return to the house.

"Dat girl ain't gwine nowhere," Abraham mumbled.

"She be in her bed sound asleep."

The young people looked at each other in wonderment.

"She's asleep in her bed?" Mandie questioned the old Negro gardener.

"Dat where she be," he replied. "Miz Taft, she send me to tell y'all."

Joe shook his head. "Of all the crazy things!" he exclaimed.

"Dat Hilda, she's a slick 'un," Liza commented.

"Oh, I feel like getting hold of her and shaking her until she tells where she's been," Mandie said as they walked toward the house.

While Abraham went on to tell the others that Hilda had been found, Mandie, Joe, and Liza went inside to find out what happened.

Mandie's grandmother told them that she had found a shawl that Hilda had left in the living room that afternoon, and she took it upstairs to Hilda's room. And there was Hilda, asleep in her bed. Since the girl couldn't talk, or wouldn't, there was no way to solve the mystery of where she had been.

Mrs. Taft invited Jake and Ludie Burns to stay for supper that evening, and they gratefully accepted. Liza escorted Hilda downstairs for the meal, and all the tired, hungry searchers ate almost everything on the table for supper.

Since there was no word from Elizabeth and John Shaw or the Woodards, they weren't expected to be home that night.

After supper, with Grandmother Taft's permission, Joe and Mandie went up to the attic again, this time to find Christmas decorations for the Burnses. As they rummaged through drawers and trunks, they filled a box with all kinds of decorations for Jake and Ludie. Then they filled another box with the things they wanted to use to decorate the Shaws' Christmas tree.

Downstairs, they found the adults and Hilda gathered in the parlor. Mrs. Taft had Hilda sitting beside her on the settee. Mandie walked over to the chair where Mr. Burns was sitting and handed him the box of decorations they had chosen for him and Ludie. Then she sat on a small stool by the fireplace while Joe stood beside her.

Jake Burns thanked Mandie awkwardly. "I think we better be gittin' home," he said. "It's gittin' awfully bad out there now."

Mrs. Taft spoke up. "Why don't you and Ludie just spend the night here?" she said. "There are plenty of rooms. And then you can travel home in the daylight."

Jake and Ludie glanced at each other uncertainly.

Jason Bond also urged them to stay. "After all, you were delayed by helping us hunt for Hilda," he said. "Otherwise you'd have been home before dark."

Ludie Burns smiled. "Well, if you think it'll be all right with Mr. Shaw . . ." she said.

"Of course," Mrs. Taft assured them. "Don't worry about it." She turned to her granddaughter. "Amanda, will you ask Liza to get a room ready for Mr. and Mrs. Burns for the night?"

Mandie smiled at the old couple. "I'm glad you're going to stay all night," she said. "Now you can help us decorate our tree."

"I 'spect I'd better go put our horse and wagon in your barn or someplace," Jake Burns said, rising from his chair. "That way our tree won't freeze."

Mr. Bond stood. "I'll help you," he said. "Let's get our

coats. Then when we get back, I'll get you to help us get our tree up." He led the way to the hall as Jake Burns nodded agreeably.

Mandie got up from the stool by the fireplace. "We'll have the tree all decorated when Mother and Uncle John get back," she said excitedly. "I'll get Liza to fix up that room, Grandmother."

Mandie found Liza eating her supper in the kitchen with Aunt Lou, Jenny the cook, and Abraham, who was Jenny's husband. Mandie stopped just inside the kitchen doorway. "Liza," she began, "Grandmother has asked Mr. and Mrs. Burns to spend the night since it's late and the weather is so bad. So she told me to ask you to get a room ready for them." She smiled. "And then as soon as you get that done, I'd like for you all to come in the parlor and help us decorate the Christmas tree."

Aunt Lou beamed. "Bless you, my chile," she said. "This gwine to be a real Christmas this year."

"My first Christmas with my mother," Mandie replied.

"And our first real Christmas in years and years," Aunt Lou said. "Ain't been nobody here to celebrate Christmas with. Mr. Shaw, he always go off somewheres on a trip."

"He always give us our presents and big pay raises befo' he go, though," Liza added.

Mandie looked around the kitchen. "I sure hope he and my mother get home soon," she said. "Nobody will tell me what my mother's big surprise for me is."

Aunt Lou walked over to her. "Now you jes' git back to yo' comp'ny," she said, shooing her out the door. "We'll all come in and help wid de tree soon as we git dis heah food put away."

"Hurry up," Mandie called back over her shoulder.

Chapter 6 / Missing Presents

Joe helped Mr. Bond and Jake Burns build a wooden stand onto the bottom of the tree trunk. And finally, after much trying, they made it steady enough to stand up in the parlor.

The servants all came in and helped with the tree decorating. Hilda stayed near, eagerly watching. When she finally understood that the decorations were to be hung on the tree, she joined in the fun. Mandie showed her how a piece of sewing thread had to be looped through the top of each one and then tied to a branch of the tree.

Snowball batted the decorative balls around the room, and when Mandie took them away from him and hung them on the tree, he reached up and tried to pull them off.

Mandie laughed at the kitten. "We may *not* get this tree done tonight," she said.

Liza replaced an ornament that Snowball had pulled off the tree. "Better keep dat cat shut up in yo' room tonight, or he'll come down heah and pull all de balls off de tree," she said.

"I hadn't thought of that," Mandie admitted. "I'm glad you warned me, Liza."

Joe stood back to survey their work. "It's beginning to look pretty," he said.

"It certainly is," Mrs. Taft agreed as she watched from her chair by the fireplace.

Ludie Burns tied an ornament on the tree and said, "I think I'll jes' let y'all finish. I ain't much good at this." She joined her husband and the other adults around the fireplace.

Aunt Lou stepped back from the tree. "It's time we's quittin', too," she said. "We all got work to do."

Mandie stopped trimming the tree and looked at the Negro housekeeper. "Work, Aunt Lou?" she asked. "At this time of night?"

"Why sho'," Aunt Lou replied. "Now git along, Liza, and you too, Jenny."

Jenny took her husband's hand. "Come along, Abraham," she ordered.

"Aunt Lou!" Mandie pleaded. "You are ruining our Christmas tree trimming party. Why do y'all have to go?"

Aunt Lou motioned to the other servants to go ahead of her out of the room. "We's got sumpin' to do dat we ain't talkin' 'bout," she answered.

The adults around the fireplace looked at each other.

Joe tied another ball on the tree, and Snowball tried to pull it down. "I wouldn't go hinting at secrets, Aunt Lou," Joe said. "You know Mandie. She won't rest until she finds out what you're talking about."

"Joe Woodard!" Mandie exclaimed.

The old Negro woman just smiled at Mandie. "She find out when we gits ready fo' huh to find out," she said.

Then she hurried out of the parlor after the other servants.

"Now, what do you suppose that was all about?" Mrs. Taft said to no one in particular.

Mandie pouted. "I wish people wouldn't have secrets," she said. "Mother has some big secret for me, and now Aunt Lou and all the other servants have secrets."

"I have a secret, too," Joe teased as he helped Hilda put a decoration on the tree.

Mandie scowled at him. "Well, I think I'll just have a secret myself," she said.

Hilda moved around the tree, placing another ornament on an already full branch. "Secret," she said, smiling at Mandie.

Mandie shook her head. "Now, don't tell me you have a secret, too, Hilda."

Hilda nodded. "Secret," she repeated.

Mrs. Taft shifted in her chair by the fireplace. "Why don't we all just have a little secret?" she said. "After all, it's Christmastime."

"That's a good idea," Joe agreed, stepping back to admire his work.

Mandie straightened a bow on the tree. "There!" she exclaimed. "I think the decorating is all finished! Now all I have to do is figure out what my secret will be."

Just as she was about to sit down, the huge grandfather clock in the front hallway chimed eleven times.

"Goodness," Mrs. Taft said, "is it eleven o'clock already? I think it's time we all retire for the night. You young people should have already been in bed. You won't want to get up in the morning." She rose and motioned to Hilda. "Come on, Hilda, dear. Bedtime."

Hilda drew back when Mrs. Taft reached for her hand.

"Grandmother, why don't you let Hilda sleep with

78

me?" Mandie suggested. "That way I'll know if she gets out of bed during the night."

"I suppose that'll be all right," Mrs. Taft agreed. She turned to Mr. and Mrs. Burns. "I'll get Liza to come and show you to your room. I hope you sleep well."

"Thank you, ma'am," Ludie Burns replied. "I'm sure we will."

"Yes, ma'am," Jake added.

Mandie took Hilda's hand. "Come on, Hilda," she said. "We're going to sleep."

"Sleep," the girl repeated, allowing Mandie to lead her upstairs.

Snowball followed.

Mandie got Hilda's nightgown from the room where the girl was supposed to be sleeping and brought it to her. "Put this on," she said.

Hilda did what she was told, and Mandie put on her own nightgown as they both hovered near the warm fireplace.

"Let's get in bed," Mandie said, and together they jumped into the big featherbed and covered up with the heavy quilts. Snowball curled up on the foot of the bed and was soon asleep.

When Mandie blew out the oil lamp by the bed, Hilda giggled and wiggled around.

By the light of the fireplace, Mandie looked into the girl's dark brown eyes. "Now, Hilda, you have to go to sleep. And don't you get out of this bed until I tell you that you can. Now go to sleep."

Hilda quieted down and closed her eyes.

Mandie, wide awake herself, waited until she was sure Hilda was fast asleep; then she slipped out of bed, put on her warm robe and slippers, and put more wood on the fire. Relighting the lamp, she moved it over to a table by a big chair.

Now would be a good time to wrap some Christmas presents, she thought. Opening her trunk, she took out some of the things she had been collecting to give her family and friends for Christmas.

Mandie knew there were scissors and wrapping paper in the sewing room, so she quietly hurried down the hallway to get them. She slowly opened the sewing room door only to find an oil lamp lighting the room but no one there. Then she noticed that there was wrapping paper strewn everywhere.

"Hilda must have been in here!" she exclaimed. Stepping into the room, she gathered up an armful of the tissue paper, then grabbed the scissors and some bright ribbon from the table nearby.

Blowing out the light, Mandie crept quietly back down the hallway to her room and carefully opened the door. And she sighed again. Hilda was wide awake and sitting up in bed.

"Hilda," Mandie said, dumping her load of wrapping supplies on the rug near her trunk. "I thought you were asleep."

Hilda just smiled. Then when Mandie sat on the rug and began cutting pieces of paper to wrap the presents in, Hilda got out of bed to join her.

"You'll have to put on your robe and slippers if you're going to stay up," Mandie told her. "I'll go to your room and get them. Don't bother any of these things, now." She indicated the paper and presents.

Hilda only smiled and sat there on the rug. And when Mandie returned with the robe and slippers, Hilda was still sitting there. Once she got Hilda dressed warmly, Mandie sat down to wrap her presents.

Hilda watched Mandie's every move, and after three presents were wrapped, Hilda reached for a piece of paper and a pair of socks. Mandie smiled as the other girl laid the paper on the floor and tried to roll up the socks inside it.

"Do it like this, Hilda," Mandie said, showing her how to fold the paper. "Now, I'm wrapping all the presents for men and boys in green paper with red ribbons and all the presents for women and girls in red paper with green ribbons. Do you understand?"

"Red, green," Hilda repeated. She smiled as she managed to get the socks wrapped.

"And I have to write the names on the presents," Mandie said, reaching for a pencil on the nearby table. "Only I think I'll just use first letters like *G* for *Grandmother*, and *L* for *Liza*, and *J* for *Joe*. But then there's Jenny, too. But that's all right. I'll know which one is which because Joe's will be in green paper and Jenny's will be in red." She paused. "Uncle John's name starts with a *J*, too, but I suppose I could just put *UJ* on his. And come to think of it, I'll have to put *AL* on Aunt Lou's, so I'll be able to tell it from Liza's."

Hilda sat there, staring at Mandie, and Mandie didn't know if she understood anything she was saying or not.

Mandie handed her a bright red wool scarf from the trunk. "Here, wrap this one for me," she said. "In red paper. That's for Liza. Here. I'll cut the paper for you."

Hilda snatched the scarf, wound it around her shoulders, and paraded around the room, humming to herself.

Mandie jumped up and tried to take the scarf away from her. But Hilda backed off, holding tightly to the red scarf.

Mandie held out her hand. "Hilda, that's for Liza, not you," she explained. "Please give it to me. Please?"

Hilda wouldn't budge.

Quickly looking through the presents she was wrapping, Mandie picked out a red silk sachet and held it out to Hilda. "Give me the scarf, and I'll give you this," Mandie offered. She held the sachet up to her nose and sniffed. "Smell of this, Hilda. It smells so good."

Hilda leaned forward to look and took a deep breath. She reached for the sachet.

Mandie pulled it back. "You have to give me the scarf."

Hilda slowly removed the scarf and gave it to Mandie as she snatched the sachet with her other hand. Then she sat down on the rug near the presents and hummed to herself as she repeatedly smelled the sachet.

Mandie quickly wrapped Liza's scarf in order to get it out of sight. Then she wrapped other presents until she had a big armful to take downstairs.

She gathered them all up. "Hilda, I have to go put these under the Christmas tree," she said. "You can go with me, but we can't make any noise. Do you understand? Quiet. Secret."

"Secret," Hilda repeated, rising to follow Mandie from the room.

Mandie crept down the stairs with Hilda following. The fire in the parlor fireplace had been banked for the night, so it gave a dim light. When they got to the tree, Hilda reached to help as Mandie distributed the presents around the floor under the limbs.

"Red, green, red, green," Mandie whispered, indicating that they should alternate the colors of the packages around the tree.

"Red, green," Hilda replied in a barely audible whisper. Then they stood back to survey their work.

"It looks pretty, doesn't it?" Mandie asked softly.

Hilda nodded and smiled. "Pretty," she whispered back.

"Time to go back to bed," Mandie said, leading the way upstairs.

Back in Mandie's room, Hilda agreed to get into bed but insisted on keeping the sachet with her.

"Hilda, we don't want to smell that thing all night," Mandie said. "Here. I know. Put it under your pillow. It'll be safe there."

Finally Hilda understood. She quickly shoved the sachet under her pillow and held the pillow tight.

Mandie blew out the light and both girls soon fell asleep. It had been a long, tiring day. And Mandie was wishing the time away until her mother would come home. She wanted to know what the big surprise was.

The snow continued through the night, and when morning came, Mandie pulled back the curtain in dismay. Evidently, Liza had come in and built the fire without waking them.

"Oh, Hilda, it's still snowing," Mandie groaned. "It looks like it's six feet deep in places out there. Mother and Uncle John will never get home today!"

Hilda came and stood beside her. "Pretty," she said, pointing to the snow that floated down outside the window.

"Yes, it's beautiful," Mandie agreed, turning back toward the bed. "Let's get dressed and go downstairs. We're probably the last ones up. I didn't even hear anyone come in to build the fire for us."

When they got downstairs, everyone else was sitting

at the table in the breakfast room. Mandie greeted them all while Mrs. Taft took Hilda over to the sideboard to get her some breakfast.

Then Mandie filled her plate and sat at the table next to Joe. "I thought sure the snow would be stopped by this morning," she said.

Mr. Bond glanced up. "Looks like it's going to continue for a while anyway."

Mrs. Taft told Mrs. Burns, "Y'all are just going to have to stay until things clear up."

"We sure do appreciate your hospitality," Mrs. Burns replied, taking a sip of coffee.

Jake Burns looked up from his bacon and eggs. "Yessum," he added. "We'll be leavin' soon's the weather permits."

Mandie nudged Joe. "You're awfully quiet this morning for some reason," she teased.

Joe reached for a hot biscuit from the platter Liza had just placed on the table. "At the rate this snow is falling, I've been waiting to see when you'd realize that our parents won't be able to get back today either," he answered.

"That was the first thing I thought of when I looked out the window this morning," Mandie said sadly. She turned to talk to the caretaker. "Mr. Jason, do you think my mother and Uncle John and Joe's parents might get through the snow?"

"I'm afraid not, Missy," he replied, cutting into the piece of ham on his plate. "There'd be too big a chance of getting stuck somewhere in the snow. And I don't think your Uncle John would allow your mother to travel in such weather."

"Amanda, they may not even be ready to come back yet," Grandmother Taft reminded her. "They may still be needed. Mr. Wright could be better, but he might be worse. And I'm sure they'll stay to help in any way they can."

"I give up on the surprise," Mandie moaned. She turned back to her grits and eggs. "I'm not going to try to persuade anybody to tell me what the big secret is anymore."

Hilda stopped eating and looked up. "Secret," she said, smiling. "Red, green, red, green. Secret."

Mandie tried to hush her. "Hilda, that's our secret, remember?"

"Oh, so now you have a secret, too," Joe teased.

Mandie pursed her lips and tossed her blonde hair. She didn't say a word.

"Anyway, we know it's red and green, according to Hilda," Joe laughed.

Mandie noticed Mr. Burns drumming his fingers on the table. Then he poured himself another cup of coffee. "I reckon Hank will figure out what delayed us," he said to Mr. Bond.

"Sure," Jason Bond replied. "If he knows you went to cut a tree from Mr. Shaw's land, he'll probably know you came by here and stayed because of the snow."

"Who's Hank?" Mandie asked.

"Hank's my wife here's cousin," Jake Burns explained. "He's been ahelpin' us git the farm ready."

Mrs. Taft smiled at him. "I'm glad you've found someone to help you get started," she said.

"Yeah, without him bein' there, we would've had to try to git back last night, 'cause there's livestock to feed and Spot and Ring to take care of."

"Spot and Ring?" Mandie asked.

"They're two beautiful pups Dr. Woodard gave us," Jake said.

"Oh, I'll have to see them," Mandie said. "How old are they?"

Jake turned to Joe. "What are they? Two, three months, maybe?"

"I think they were born about October first," he said. "Mandie, remember my dog, Samantha? They're two of her last puppies."

"Oh, yes," Mandie said. "Samantha had new puppies when we stopped to visit you on our way to see my Cherokee kinspeople."

Mandie remembered that was after her father had died at Charley Gap and she had been reunited with her real mother, Elizabeth. And then Elizabeth had married Mandie's Uncle John.

"Well," Grandmother Taft said, rising from the table, "with all this snow now, I think today would be a good day for us all to get ready for Christmas. I know I have presents to wrap. And Amanda, you and Joe could get the holly, and mistletoe, and other greenery off the back porch and decorate the house. Then we'll have everything ready and waiting when your mother and the others do get home."

"All right. I'll be finished eating in a minute," she told Joe.

As the adults left the table, Hilda followed them out of the room.

"I'm going upstairs for a moment, Mandie," Joe said. "I'll meet you in the parlor."

Mandie rushed through her breakfast and then hurried out to the parlor. As she looked at the tall Christmas tree, her heart did flip-flops. Someone had taken all the red-wrapped presents from under the tree.

Who would do such a thing? she wondered. It couldn't have been Hilda. She had slept with her last night, and if Hilda had got out of bed, Mandie would have known it. So who did it, and where were all her presents for the women and girls?

Just then Joe came in and found her staring at the tree. "Ready?" he asked.

"Oh, Joe, somebody has taken all the presents I wrapped in red paper last night," she said furiously. "Look! There are only green ones left." She pointed to the bottom of the tree.

"Hilda?" Joe said immediately.

"No, Hilda slept with me, and I think I would have known if she got out of bed," Mandie replied. "In fact, we stayed up real late wrapping the presents. She helped me, and when we went to bed, we were so sleepy I don't think she would have wanted to get up again."

Joe thought for a moment. "Well, I can't imagine who else could have taken them."

"How will I ever find them?" Mandie sighed. "Now I will have to get more presents to give to Aunt Lou, Liza, Jenny, and Hilda."

"I'm sorry, Mandie," Joe tried to comfort her.

"I'm just glad I hadn't finished all my wrapping," Mandie said. "I still have some of the other presents upstairs unwrapped, like the ones for Mother, and Celia, and Morning Star, and Sallie."

"Are you expecting Uncle Ned, and Morning Star, and Sallie to come for Christmas?" Joe asked.

"Uncle Ned promised they would come some time during the holidays," Mandie explained. "He didn't know exactly when, but they'll be here."

Just then Snowball came wandering into the parlor to find his mistress, and Mandie picked him up.

"For once we can't blame this on Snowball," Joe laughed. "And you said Hilda couldn't have done it, so we'll have to do a little looking around to see if we can find the presents. I wonder why only the red ones were taken."

"I don't know," Mandie said, "but all the red ones are for the women and girls. The green ones are for the men and boys."

"In other words, the one for me is still under there?" Joe teased, stooping to look over the remaining presents.

Mandie pulled him back. "Don't you dare bother my presents!"

Joe straightened up. "Well, I'm glad I haven't put my presents under the tree yet," he said. "They might have disappeared, too."

"I think we should go talk to my grandmother," Mandie suggested.

"Let's go," Joe agreed.

Chapter 7 / Red, Green, Red, Green

When Mandie and Joe found Mrs. Taft, she was in her room wrapping her Christmas presents. She quickly laid an extra quilt over the bed where she was working, trying to hide what she had laid out there.

She was shocked when Mandie and Joe told her about the missing presents. "But, dear, it must have been Hilda," she told Mandie. "You know how she is always getting involved in unsuspected doings."

"No, Grandmother, this time I just can't believe it was Hilda," Mandie disagreed. "I know I would have heard her if she got out of bed."

"Well, it's hard to believe that anyone else in the house would do such a thing," Mrs. Taft replied. "I suppose the best thing to do is to start looking for the presents."

"And what am I going to do if we don't find them?" Mandie whined. "I'll have to get to a store somehow to replace the ones that were taken."

"I think you'll find them somewhere in the house, dear," said Grandmother Taft. "No one has come in or left since you put them there."

Joe ran his fingers through his brown hair. "I don't

think we ought to ask anyone else to help us, though," he said. "The fewer people who know about this the better since we don't know who is guilty."

"You're right, Joe," Mandie agreed. "Let's start looking."

"Start with Hilda's room, just in case," Mrs. Taft suggested. "As soon as I wrap these presents I'll see if I can help you."

"I wouldn't put those presents under the tree if I were you," Joe said.

"Oh, I think they would be all right," Mrs. Taft replied. "But I won't put them under the tree for the next day or two until I get them all wrapped anyway."

Mandie and Joe turned to leave the room. "We'll let you know if we find them, Grandmother," Mandie said.

As they began their search, Mandie knew it would be a big task to look in all the rooms, in all the drawers and wardrobes and anything that could hold such stuff. But they followed Grandmother Taft's advice and started with Hilda's room first.

Hilda followed them up the stairs and into her room.

"Hilda, have you seen all the presents we wrapped in red paper?" Mandie asked as she looked all over in the room. "Remember, we put them under the tree last night?"

Hilda smiled at her. "Red, green, red, green," she said.

"It's no use," Joe said with a shrug. "She doesn't understand what you're talking about, and I can't find anything."

"Hilda, you stay here," Mandie said. "Take a nap. Sleep. We'll be back soon."

Hilda only stood there smiling. And when they left the room, she followed, sticking right with them as they searched. Snowball showed up now and then, too. When they started up the stairs to the attic, the white kitten ran ahead and sat there waiting for them to open the door and let him in.

"Snowball, what are you up to?" Mandie asked.

Joe reached forward and opened the door. "He probably smells a mouse," he said as the kitten rushed past him into the dark attic.

With the snow still falling outside and no sunshine, the attic windows didn't let in much light.

"I'd better get the lamp from the hallway down there," Joe said, turning to go back down.

Hilda rushed past him and ran downstairs.

Joe frowned in confusion but brought the lamp back up and lit it.

"That's better," Mandie said, looking around.

"It seems like we've been through all this stuff up here so many times," Joe remarked as they searched through the furniture.

"And every time we find something we hadn't found before," Mandie replied, stooping to inspect a huge wooden box. "I wonder what this is. I don't remember seeing it before."

"I wouldn't open that if I were you," Joe advised. "You see that lettering on the side?" He pointed to the crude letters. "It says, Pryvit Propity of Abraham."

"Private property of Abraham?" Mandie questioned, examining the box. "I wonder what it is." She tried to pick it up, but it was too heavy. "Why do you suppose Abraham put some of his private property up here in Uncle John's attic when he has his own house in the yard out there?"

"Maybe it's something for Jenny for Christmas," Joe replied, lifting the box. "Or it could be some things he didn't have room for in his house now that Jenny has come back to live with him again."

"Probably. I hope Jenny stays with her husband this time," Mandie said, continuing her search for the missing presents. "That sure hasn't been a happy marriage."

"That's because they didn't trust each other for all those years. But now, maybe that's all cleared up," Joe remarked. "When we get old enough to get married, I think ours will be a happy marriage."

Mandie stopped examining a drawer in a chest and straightened up. "I'm not certain that we'll ever get married, Joe. I wish you'd remember that. When we are older we might meet someone else or change our minds," she reminded him.

"I know you talk like that, Mandie, but I think we will grow up and get married, especially after I get your father's house back for you like I promised." He sat down on top of an old trunk.

"I know I promised I'd marry you someday if you'd get my father's house back for me when we grow up, but you can't hold me to that promise always," Mandie protested. "Like I said, we may both change our minds."

"I picked some mistletoe and some holly with bright red berries and put it on your father's grave before we came," Joe told her.

"Oh, Joe, I appreciate that so much." Mandie's blue eyes filled with tears. "Last Christmas I was with my father back there in Charley Gap. Now this Christmas I'll be with my mother here. I just wish we could have all been together for a little while."

"The Lord knows best, Mandie," Joe said softly. He patted her small white hand. "Just be thankful for the years you did have with your father."

Mandie pulled her hand free to brush away her tears. "Well . . ." She turned to a nearby wardrobe and flung open the door. "We've just got to find those presents!"

"We will," Joe assured her as he began looking into some of the trunks around him.

"Or we'll have to dig a path to the stores downtown so I can buy more," Mandie told him.

Snowball sniffed around the attic awhile; then Mandie saw him run back down the stairs.

"At least Snowball went downstairs now, so we don't have to look for him in all this mess," she said. "I wonder where Hilda went."

As it turned out, no one seemed to know where Hilda had gone. When Joe and Mandie found no presents in the attic, they went back downstairs and discovered that Hilda was missing again. Although they looked all over the house, they couldn't find her or Snowball.

"I think Hilda has learned to play games with us," Joe said. "She has found some way to hide where we can't find her."

"And she must have taken Snowball with her," Mandie added.

After giving up on finding the girl, they joined the others in the parlor. Mrs. Taft had finished wrapping her presents for the time being, and she was sitting near the fireplace with Mr. Bond and the Burnses.

"Maybe if we'd just stop looking for her every time she disappears, she'd quit hiding from us," Jason Bond suggested.

"That would be hard to do since we don't know if she has gone outside or not," Mandie said. "Then, too, Snowball must be with her."

"If she had gone outside, we'd find her footprints in the snow," Joe reasoned.

As the grandfather clock in the hall struck twelve noon, Mrs. Taft stood up. "It's time for dinner now," she said. "And Hilda's not here to eat."

At that moment Liza appeared in the doorway. "Dinner be put on de table," she announced, "and dat Hilda girl be sittin' at de table, waitin'."

Everyone looked at each other. Mandie started into the dining room with the others. Where had Hilda been? And how did she know it was time to eat?

Mandie caught up with Liza on the way to the dining room. "Where did Hilda come from? Which direction?" she asked.

"I don't rightly know, Missy," Liza replied. "Me and Jenny and Aunt Lou was dishin' up de food in de kitchen, and in she walks with dat white cat of yours."

"Where is Snowball now?" Mandie asked.

"He havin' his dinner in de kitchen," Liza told her, dancing on ahead to help serve.

As they all sat around the huge dining room table, everyone tried to ask Hilda questions, but she only smiled and did not answer.

Joe spoke softly to Mandie so no one else could hear. "Well, I suppose we can go ahead and decorate with the holly and mistletoe this afternoon," he said.

Mandie took a long drink of water from the glass by her plate. "If we can hurry and get that done, then we can look some more for my presents," she whispered back.

"Look where?" Joe asked quietly. "We've looked the whole house over."

They continued talking in whispers because they didn't want anyone to know that they had missed the presents. But Mandie noticed that Hilda was watching them closely, and she wondered if the girl could read lips.

"We're being eavesdropped on," Mandie said softly, glancing at Hilda.

Joe nodded and fell silent.

Mr. Bond looked out the tall French windows at the high snowdrifts outside. "That snow just keeps on out there," he said. "I don't believe I've ever seen it snow this much for so long without letting up for a while."

"Me neither," Jake Burns agreed.

"I do wish it'd clear up enough for Elizabeth and the others to get home," Mrs. Taft remarked. "At the rate it's going, they may not be able to make it home in time for Christmas Day."

Mandie dropped her fork onto her plate. "Mother not here for Christmas?" she exclaimed. "She's got to get here for Christmas!"

"I'm sure she'll do her best to get back by then, but you might as well be prepared in case she doesn't," Grandmother Taft warned. "Don't get your hopes up too much. That weather is bad out there, and it could be a lot worse over at Tellico, where they are."

As Mandie thought about Christmas without her mother, she couldn't eat another bite. "Celia Hamilton and her mother are supposed to come in time for News Year's Day," Mandie reminded her grandmother. "Do you think they might not make it either?"

"I just don't know," Mrs. Taft said. "They'll be coming by train. Your mother and the others went in the rig."

"At least there's one I can always count on," Mandie said. "Uncle Ned will be here no matter what kind of weather we have."

Joe sat forward. "You said he didn't tell you what day, though," he said.

"No, but that's all right. He'll be here sooner or later,"

Mandie replied. "He promised my father he would watch over me, and he always does." Her voice trembled.

Grandmother Taft took a sip of coffee. "If you young people are finished, you may be excused," she said.

Mandie and Joe hurried out to the back porch, which was partially enclosed. Hilda trailed along behind them, stopping in the doorway. There were piles of holly with bright red berries and bunches of mistletoe. Some were covered with a little snow where it had blown in.

"Brr! It's cold out here!" Mandie exclaimed, shivering in the cold air.

Joe gathered up some of the limbs. "We should have put on our coats," he agreed.

"Move back, Hilda," Mandie said, grabbing an armload of branches. "We're going to bring this inside."

Hilda stepped aside as Mandie and Joe carried the greenery into the hallway and divided it up, taking some of it into the parlor. Without saying a word Hilda watched and tried to help. They made wreaths out of some of it and hung them in the windows. And they placed a huge wreath on the outside of the front door.

As Hilda played with the berries from the holly, she kept saying, "Red, green, red, green."

Mandie stopped working a moment. "Hilda, why do you keep saying that?"

"Do you know what happened to all the presents wrapped in red paper that were under the Christmas tree?" Joe asked.

Hilda grinned mischievously and started humming to herself.

"Are you sure it couldn't have been her?" Joe questioned Mandie.

"I'm sure," Mandie answered. "I do have some other ideas about it, though."

"Like who else could have taken them?"

Mandie nodded as she tied a red bow on a wreath they had made.

"Who?" Joe asked softly.

"We can't talk right now," Mandie cautioned.

After all the wreaths were hung, they looked around the first floor of the house, trying to decide where to hang the mistletoe.

"Definitely one piece over the front door," Joe said, laughing. "That'll catch anyone who comes through."

"People won't look up and see it. Are you going to stand here and tell them it's there?" Mandie asked, laughing with him.

"We'll hang it low enough so they can't miss it," Joe answered. "I'll go find a tack and the hammer."

Mandie tied red bows on some of the mistletoe and stuck it around in various places. Then Joe came back with a stepladder and climbed up to fasten the mistletoe over the doorway.

"Let's do the back door, too," Mandie said excitedly.

"All right," Joe agreed.

After they decorated the back door, Joe reached out and opened the door to see if it cleared the mistletoe. And suddenly he came face-to-face with a stranger on the porch, who was stomping snow from his feet.

"This John Shaw's house?" the stranger asked, brushing snow from his clothes.

Mandie came and stood beside Joe. "Yes, it is," she said. "Who are you?"

"I wasn't sure this was the right house. I'm kinda new in town," the man said. "I have a message here that came over the telegraph this morning." He fumbled in his pocket.

"A message? Who is it for?" Joe asked.

"Joe, we need to invite the man inside," Mandie said, stepping back into the hallway.

"Of course, come on inside," Joe said. "In fact, come into the kitchen, and we'll find you something hot to drink." He led the way through the doorway into the kitchen.

"Thank you very kindly," the man said.

The warmth from the huge iron cookstove felt good as they slipped through the doorway. All the servants were having their meal at the table by the big fireplace at one end.

Aunt Lou looked up as they came in. "And who dat what be crazy 'nuff to come out in dis snow?" she teased.

"Aunt Lou, he has a message from the telegraph for us," Mandie explained as the stranger continued to fumble in his many pockets. "Could somebody please give him a hot drink so he can warm up before he has to go back out in this weather?"

Mandie turned back to the man, who finally found the piece of paper. He handed it to Mandie.

"Why, this is addressed to me!" she exclaimed, examining the paper.

Joe crowded close to read over her shoulder, but Mandie was so excited she was moving around too much for him to be able to read anything. Hilda stood nearby, looking confused.

"It's from my mother!" Mandie gasped. "Imagine hearing from my mother by the telegraph!"

"Well, stand still and read it," Joe said impatiently. "What does it say?"

" 'Darling daughter,' " Mandie read, " 'Mr. Wright, our dear friend, has passed on. We will stay until everything is taken care of, but we will all be home in time for Christmas, no matter what the weather. I love you. Mother.' "

Mandie stood there speechless as she squeezed the piece of paper in her hand. Then she started jumping up and down. "I knew it! I knew she would get home in time for Christmas! Oh, I've got to tell Grandmother."

Joe and Hilda followed as she raced through the hallway, calling loudly for her grandmother.

She found all the adults in the parlor. "Grandmother! They'll all be here for Christmas!" she cried, thrusting the piece of paper into the woman's hand.

Mrs. Taft, alarmed at the excitement, took the paper and read it aloud while the others listened.

"That means my parents will be back in time for Christmas, too," Joe said with a big grin.

Mandie quickly turned to Joe. "Oh, forgive me for thinking only of *my* mother, Joe," she said. "Of course you were anxious for your parents to get back, too. I'm so glad." She reached for Joe's hand and gave it a little squeeze.

Mr. Bond looked concerned. "I don't want to ruin your happiness," he said, "but please remember, this snow has got to stop before anyone can get through from Tellico."

"I know, but I figure God will turn it all off tonight so my mother can come home in time to celebrate Jesus' birthday with me," Mandie said with tears of joy sparkling in her blue eyes.

Ludie Burns sat forward. "Bless you, child. I hope so," she said.

"I hope so, too," her husband added, "so we can be gittin' on home ourselves."

Suddenly Hilda ran over to Mrs. Taft, knelt by her chair

and threw her arms around her. "Mother!" she said to everyone's surprise.

Mrs. Taft hugged her back. "Yes, Hilda, darling," Mrs. Taft said. "I'll be your mother. I love you."

Then just as suddenly, Hilda jumped up and started dancing around the Christmas tree, saying, "Red, green, red, green," in a sing-song fashion.

Mandie couldn't help but wonder why Hilda kept saying that if she had nothing to do with the missing presents.

That night, before Mandie crawled into bed, she knelt with Hilda by the fire to say her prayers. "Thank you, dear God, for letting me hear from my mother. But please, don't you think we've had enough snow?" she prayed. "Please make sure my mother and all the others get home in time to celebrate Jesus' birthday. Thank you, dear God. Thank you for everything and everybody."

Hilda tried to repeat what Mandie was saying, but finally she just said, "Thank. God."

Mandie hugged the girl and they quickly crawled into the warm featherbed and pulled the heavy quilts over them.

Just before she dropped off to sleep Mandie's last thoughts were, *My mother will be home for Christmas. And now I can find out what the big surprise is.*

Chapter 8 / Mysterious Footprints

The next thing Mandie knew, Liza was shaking her awake.

"Missy, better git up and go look under de Christmas tree," Liza said.

Mandie's eyes opened wide, and she jumped out of bed. "What's wrong now, Liza?"

Startled by Mandie's sudden movement, Snowball hopped down and ran out the open door.

"I hates to tell you dis, Missy," Liza said, stirring up the fire she had just built in the fireplace, "but all dem red presents, dey be back under de tree, and de green ones dey be gone now."

"Oh, no!" Mandie shrieked so loudly that Hilda woke up and jumped out of bed.

"Secret?" Hilda asked, joining them by the fire.

Mandie ignored Hilda. "What else is going to happen?" She sighed.

"Dat ain't all. No it ain't," Liza said.

"Liza, come on and tell me," Mandie begged. "What is it?"

"Well, it be like dis," the little maid replied. "All dem

presents be back, but somebody done messed 'em all up."

"Messed them all up? How?" she asked, slipping into her robe and helping Hilda with hers. "I'll just go see."

As she hurried down the stairs, Liza and Hilda followed. Down in the parlor beneath the Christmas tree, they found all Mandie's red-wrapped presents, but the paper and ribbons were all wrinkled. And now all the green presents were missing.

Tears came to Mandie's eyes as she stooped down to pick up some of the presents and examine them. Hilda stood back.

"How could anybody do this to me?" Mandie said as the tears ran down her cheeks.

Liza stooped beside her. "Missy, I'll help you put new paper on all dem presents," she said. "We kin fix 'em up all pretty agin."

"But, Liza, whoever did this found out everything I had wrapped up, and it was all my secret," Mandie said with a catch in her voice.

"Secret. Secret," Hilda said, walking around the tree.

Mandie ignored her. "Liza, would you please help me carry all these things back to my room?" she asked. "And after we have breakfast I would appreciate it if you'd help me rewrap everything."

"I sho' will," the Negro girl said, piling her arms full of presents.

The two carried the packages to Mandie's room while Hilda followed, watching. Mandie opened her trunk and put them all inside, then shut the lid.

When Mandie saw Hilda watching, she picked up a dress nearby. "We have to get dressed and go downstairs for breakfast, Hilda," she said. "Thank you for your help, Liza."

Liza danced over to the door and started to leave, but then she stopped. "I be seein' you after breakfus'," she said, closing the door behind her as she left the room.

Then the door opened again, and Liza stuck her head back inside the room. "Missy, what we goin' to do 'bout all dem green presents dat's missin'?" she asked.

"I don't know, Liza," Mandie replied, pulling her dress over her head. "I suppose we'll have to look for them. But Joe and I looked the whole house over before, and we couldn't find the red ones." She paused and then looked at Liza, questioningly. "How did you know the red-wrapped presents were missing, anyway?" she asked. "We didn't tell anybody except Grandmother."

"I got eyes, ain't I?" Liza laughed. "You got eyes, too. Draw dat curtain and look outside." She closed the door quickly and left.

Mandie ran to the window and drew the draperies. Bright sunshine poured into the room. And although there was plenty of snow on the ground, there was not a single snowflake in the air.

"Oh, thank you, dear God!" she cried excitedly, looking up into the beautiful blue sky. "I knew you'd stop the snow so my mother and the others could come home for Jesus' birthday." Then she sighed as she looked across the deep snowdrifts. "I wonder if it's warm enough to melt all that snow," she said to herself.

Hilda joined her at the window, and when Mandie turned to look at her, she saw that Hilda had put on her dress backward. The tiny buttons that were supposed to be on the back of the bodice were in front.

"Hilda, we have to take off your dress and turn it around," Mandie said, smiling.

Hilda moved away from her and crossed her arms over her chest.

"Come on, Hilda, you can't wear the dress like that," Mandie scolded as she tried to get near enough to un-button Hilda's dress.

"No!" Hilda screamed. And she ran out the door into the hallway.

Mandie quickly finished dressing, gave a quick brush-ing to her long blonde hair, and went after Hilda. But she couldn't find her. Thinking the girl had gone on down to breakfast, Mandie hurried to the breakfast room. Every-one else was there except Hilda.

"Did Hilda come in here?" Mandie asked after greet-ing everyone quickly.

"Don't tell me that girl is missing again," Joe moaned.

"Amanda, dear, don't you know where she is?" Grand-mother Taft asked.

Ludie Burns looked up from her plate. "That's the beatingest girl I ever seed for disappearing," she said.

"Well, this time I'm not going to worry about her," Mandie said, taking a plate and filling it at the sideboard. "I'm going to eat my breakfast right now."

Mr. Bond laughed. "Good idea. She's around here somewhere," he said.

"I really think she's just playing games with us," Joe said, biting into a piece of crisp bacon. "She likes us to hunt for her."

"Well, we won't this time," Mrs. Taft announced as Liza filled her coffee cup.

Mandie sat down next to Joe with her plate full.

"I take it you've already looked outside," Joe said.

Mandie smiled. "I certainly have," she replied. "It looks wonderful out there this morning. Mr. Jason, do you think it's warm enough to melt all that snow?"

"Well," the caretaker replied, "maybe later in the day.

We'll get it all dug off the driveway and walkway, though."

"May I help?" Mandie asked, excited at the prospect of going outside.

"Me, too?" Joe added quickly.

Mr. Bond looked across the table at Mrs. Taft.

Mrs. Taft nodded. "I suppose it will be all right if you young people wrap up real good and don't stay out too long," she said. "I certainly don't want to be responsible for letting you two get bad colds."

"Thank you, Grandmother. We'll put on our heaviest coats and boots," Mandie promised, hurrying to finish her breakfast.

Liza walked around the table, refilling coffee cups. "Want me to he'p, too?" she asked. "We could make one of dem snowmen things."

Joe brightened. "That's a great idea, Liza."

Mrs. Taft pushed her empty plate aside. "You may help them clear the pathways, Liza," she said. "And then you young people may build a snowman if you have time before noon."

"Thank you, ma'am," Liza said. "I goes and tells Aunt Lou you say fo' me to he'p dig de snow out."

"Liza, tell Aunt Lou I also gave you permission to go ahead and eat your breakfast now so you can help outside," Mrs. Taft called to her across the room. "Now hurry and get finished."

Liza scurried out to the kitchen.

"Thanks, Grandmother," Mandie said. "Aunt Lou probably wouldn't allow Liza to help us unless you said so."

"I'm not exactly the lady of the house, but since your mother is not here, and I am her mother, I thought perhaps I could use a little influence," Mrs. Taft said, laughing.

With Joe's help, Mandie quickly searched the house for the missing presents while Liza was eating her breakfast. But they found nothing. Then the presents were forgotten as they got involved in the snow shoveling.

"Grandmother said she would ask the servants to help her look for Hilda again while the others were outside," Mandie said.

When Jason Bond opened the back screen door, the young people saw Abraham shoveling a wider pathway from his house in the back yard to the Shaws' big house. There was already a narrow trail between the huge drifts, which he evidently made so that Jenny could get back and forth to do the Shaws' cooking.

"Good morning, Abraham!" Mandie called across the yard. "We're going to help you."

"Mawnin', Missy," Abraham replied, stopping to lean on his shovel. "I be right glad to git some he'p. I sho' will."

Jason Bond gave out the shovels that had been pushed up under the back porch out of the snow. Since the mountains of western North Carolina were always filled with snow and ice, Mr. Bond kept an adequate supply of tools for digging out.

Mandie stood on the back porch steps and took the shovel he handed her. "Mr. Jason, why don't I go back through the house and start on the front walkway?" she offered.

"Yes," Joe said. "Mandie and I could get the front done in no time."

"All right," Mr. Bond agreed. "Now don't waste time doing any extra shoveling to the sides. Just make a straight bee line down the front walk. Then if we have time, we'll spread out wider."

Liza stayed in back to help since that area was a lot larger.

Mandie and Joe hurried back through the house to the front door, and when they opened it, they found most of the front porch covered with snow.

As Mandie pushed the screen door open, she gasped. "Look, Joe!" She pointed to deep footprints across the porch.

Joe joined her. "Looks to me like all the footprints are headed up toward the front door," he said, "and whoever made them didn't go back out again."

"You're right," Mandie agreed. "But nobody has come in since it started snowing."

"The messenger from the telegraph office . . ." Joe began, "but then he came in the back door, didn't he?"

"Yes, he did."

"And Abraham goes in and out the back door."

"What could all this mean?" Mandie was puzzled. "I'd say they were made by a man's shoes, wouldn't you?"

"A large pair of shoes, yes," Joe agreed. "Well, are we going to get to work shoveling or not?"

Mandie picked up her shovel. "Why don't we just shovel around these footprints for the time being?" she suggested. "That way, we can show them to Mr. Bond later."

"All right," Joe said. "Since they are so near the edge of the steps, we'll still be able to clear enough snow away to make a path." He thrust his shovel into the snow and tossed a load out into the side of the yard.

"We're going to have to be careful working so close together," Mandie cautioned, "or we'll hit each other with the handles of our shovels." She pitched a shovelful of snow off the other side of the porch.

"You take one side, and I'll take the other," he said. "Give me a minute to get a few steps ahead of you. Then we won't bang into each other."

Mandie waited until he had cleaned one side of the wide front porch steps, and then she began shoveling the other side, being careful to preserve the large footprints in the snow.

They made rapid progress down the walkway toward the road, tossing the snow into the yard as they went. As they neared the gate, they could see tracks in the snow where at least one wagon had gone through.

"I suppose when we get the driveway cleaned out at the back, we'll be able to get the wagon into the street," Mandie remarked, looking down the road.

Joe came over to her side to glance outside the gate. "I wouldn't want to get a wagon out into that road," he said. "Look how deep the snow is."

"I heard Grandmother ask the Burnses to stay over another night because she thought they might not be able to get all the way to their house," Mandie said, resuming her shoveling.

"And they don't live very far from here," Joe answered, flipping a shovelful of snow into the yard. "There's just too much snow on the roads today.'"

"It's melting fast, though," Mandie observed. "Look how soft it is, and it's all runny underneath." She demonstrated.

"Today's Saturday. Maybe by Monday our folks will be able to get back," Joe remarked.

Mandie straightened up. "Monday!" she cried. "Christmas Day is Tuesday!"

"If they get back on Monday, I'll consider them lucky with all this snow," Joe said.

"But Mother's message said they would be back in time for Christmas," Mandie moaned.

"Well, if they get back on Monday, that'll be in time for Christmas," Joe reminded her.

"Barely," Mandie answered.

Just then Snowball came bounding down the pathway they had dug from the front porch. He was shaking his paws as he went, trying to get rid of the trace of snow sticking to them.

"Look who's here," Joe said.

"Snowball!" Mandie scolded as the kitten ran playfully after her shovel. "How did you get out of the house?"

The white cat tried to rub around her legs, but Mandie shoved him away. "You're all wet," she fussed. "Quit that!"

"Looks like we've finished the walkway," Joe said, surveying the long clear path to the porch. "Shall we go outside the gate and clear a place to tether the horses in case someone comes before it all melts?"

"Oh yes, let's do," Mandie urged. "Let's hurry and finish, and then we can get Liza and build a snowman."

After completing their task, with Snowball roaming around and meowing, Mandie ran up on the front porch, removed her wet boots, and hurried through the house to find Liza. The little Negro maid was still helping in the back, but she was thrilled to begin having some fun.

As the two girls put their boots back on outside the front door, Mandie showed Liza the large footprints she and Joe had preserved in the snow.

"But dey don't go no place, Missy," Liza said, stooping to look.

"You mean whoever it was didn't come in the house?" Mandie asked. "I know. We haven't had any visitors through the front door. I think we have another mystery on our hands."

"But look, dey start out there at de summerhouse." Liza pointed across the yard. "Where did dey come from to git there?"

"You know, you're right," Joe said, joining them on the porch. "The footprints start from the summerhouse and end here on the porch, but there aren't any footprints going back out."

Mandie sighed. "We didn't think about that, did we?" she said. "I don't think anyone could have stayed in the summerhouse all this time during the snowstorm. And once they got to the front door, what did they do?"

"Come on," Joe told the girls. "Let's get started on the snowman while we talk. Otherwise Mandie's grand-mother may be calling us in pretty soon. We've been out here awhile already."

They shoveled a rough path through the deep snow to the center of the yard, and there they began shaping a snowman, throwing snowballs at each other now and then. Snowball kept out of their way.

Liza stopped a moment to look at the footprints across the yard. "Reckon dat musta been some ghost man dat made dem footprints," she remarked.

"And he must've been coming after you, Liza," Joe teased. "Maybe he just couldn't get the door open."

Liza stared at him in fright. "I d-don't know no ghost man," she stammered. "He not comin' to see me. He comin' to see you."

"Maybe Mr. Jason or Abraham can help us figure out where he went," Mandie suggested.

Joe packed a large handful of snow onto the snow-man's head. "They can't figure out anything any more than we can," he said. "The footprints are there, going one way, and that's all."

"Don't be too sure about that, Joe," Mandie replied. "Somebody is bound to know who made them."

But Joe was right. Later, when the young people showed the footprints to Jason Bond, Abraham, and Jake Burns, they were all puzzled, too. No one had any ideas about the strange prints.

Chapter 9 / More Missing Presents

The young people didn't wait for Mrs. Taft to call them back into the house. Even though they had built up some warmth while they were shoveling snow, they had become cold while building the snowman. So after showing the strange footprints to the men, they voluntarily sought the warmth of the indoors. They took off their snow-wet boots just outside the front door and carried them to the kitchen to dry.

"You gotta see our snowman, Aunt Lou," Mandie told the big Negro housekeeper, who was directing activities in the warm kitchen.

"I ain't got time to look at no snowman, my chile," Aunt Lou replied, bustling about. "You jes' git right upstairs now and change dem wet clothes 'fo' you gits a cold and yo' mama come home blamin' me now, you hear?"

"I hear, Aunt Lou," Mandie said, removing her heavy coat. "But my clothes aren't wet, just my shoes."

Aunt Lou bent over and caught Mandie's skirt at the hem. "Dat skirt be wet round de bottom," she said. "Now you gits upstairs right now and git dem clothes changed, my chile."

Mandie smiled. "Yes, ma'am, I will, if you say so," she replied.

Aunt Lou looked over at Joe and Liza, who were warming themselves by the huge iron cookstove. "Now you do de same, you hear?" she admonished. "Liza, you gits yo' dress changed and git back in heah to work. Right now."

Liza scurried toward the kitchen door as Aunt Lou started fussing at Joe. "And you, doctuh's son, just 'cause yo' pa be a doctuh ain't no sign he got time to be adoctorin' you when he got all dem other sick folks to look after."

Joe laughed. "All right, Aunt Lou, I'll change, too," he said, following Mandie and Liza out of the room.

Liza met the other two in the hallway. "Race you up de steps!" she whispered. And instantly she took off, running up the stairs.

Mandie and Joe followed, but Liza had a head start. Although her room was on the third floor, she stopped on the second-floor landing. "Beat you!" she called back to them. Then she started up the next flight of stairs, walking.

"Oh, well," Mandie said as she reached the landing.

Joe was right with her. "The steps aren't wide enough for the three of us to run together," he said. "That's why you won, Liza."

At that moment Hilda came running down the stairs past Liza.

"Heah be dat Hilda girl," she called to Mandie and Joe as she continued on upstairs.

Mandie frowned. "Hilda, where have you been?" she asked, stopping her. "Your room is on the second floor here with ours. What were you doing up on the third floor?"

Hilda smiled and turned at the landing to hurry down the second-floor hallway.

"Save your breath, Mandie," Joe said. "She has no idea what you're saying."

They started toward their rooms. "I'm not so sure she doesn't understand," Mandie replied. "It may be that she understands but still doesn't know how to talk very well." She opened the door to her room. "Anyway, see you downstairs."

Closing the door behind her, Mandie looked around the room, expecting to see Hilda there. But she wasn't. Mandie quickly looked into the room that Hilda was supposed to be occupying, and there she was, sitting in the middle of the bed, playing with Snowball.

"Hilda, why don't you come into my room while I change clothes," she offered. She wanted to keep Hilda in sight so she wouldn't have to go looking for her when the noon meal was announced.

Hilda looked at her and smiled but didn't budge. Mandie walked over and took her hand to entice her to come along. Snowball jumped down to the floor, but Hilda still didn't move.

"I have another secret, Hilda," Mandie said.

"Secret," Hilda repeated. And she jumped down from the bed.

Then Mandie noticed that Hilda was not wearing the same dress she had put on backward that morning. This dress was made with the buttons in the front, and she had it on right.

"Yes, I have another secret," Mandie told her. "Let's go to my room."

She didn't have any trouble getting Hilda to follow her. Mandie's room was on the front of the house, so when they got to her room, she pointed out the window. "See the snowman?"

Hilda stared out the window.

"That's the secret I wanted to show you," Mandie said. "Joe and Liza and I made it."

Hilda turned to Mandie. "Secret?" she asked.

"Part of the secret is some big, big footprints on the front porch," Mandie continued. "They come from the summerhouse. We don't know who made them, so it's somebody's secret." She turned to the chifferobe and took out a dress.

Hilda seemed to be puzzled. "Secret," she repeated the word as she gazed out the window. Then as Mandie started changing clothes, Hilda watched her put on a clean dress, stockings, and dry slippers.

Snowball sat by the fireplace washing his damp white fur; then he curled up on the rug and went to sleep.

"I think it's about time to eat, Hilda," Mandie said, tying back her long blonde hair with a ribbon. "Let's go downstairs."

Hilda followed Mandie downstairs and into the parlor. There Grandmother Taft and Mrs. Burns sat by the fireplace while Mr. Burns and Jason Bond stood in front of the fire, warming themselves. Joe was looking out the window at the snowman in the front yard.

"I hope y'all didn't get too much of that cold out there, Amanda," her grandmother said.

"I don't think so," Mandie replied. She took a seat on the settee, and Hilda plopped onto a stool by the fireplace. "When did Hilda show up? Did you change her dress?"

"Why, she came into the breakfast room right after y'all went out to shovel snow," Mrs. Taft replied. She looked at Hilda. "And that's the same dress she's had on all morning as far as I know."

"No, Grandmother, she had on a pink dress that buttoned down the back this morning," Mandie explained. "She put it on backward and wouldn't let me change it. I suppose that's why she disappeared."

Ludie Burns spoke up. "I seen her come out of her room when I went up to our room after breakfast," she said, "and that's the dress she had on then."

"I was still at the table when she came in, and I made sure she ate her breakfast," Mrs. Taft added.

Joe walked across the room from the window and sat down in a nearby chair. "Mrs. Taft, did Mr. Bond and Mr. Burns tell you about the mysterious footprints we found out there on the front porch?" he asked.

"Yes, they mentioned something about some odd footprints, I believe," she replied. "Perhaps someone knocked on the door, and we didn't hear them, so they went away."

"But the prints don't go back out. They only head in toward the front door," Joe explained.

"They come from the summerhouse and don't show up anywhere else," Mandie added.

"Secret," Hilda said, humming to herself.

Mandie looked at the girl and smiled, remembering that she had told Hilda that the footprints were a secret.

Just then Liza came in and stood in the doorway. "Dinner be on de table," she announced.

Everyone got up and started to leave the room to go to the dining room. Liza waited until Mandie and Joe passed through the doorway, then she whispered, "And there ain't no ghost man 'spected fo' dinner."

"You might just be surprised," Joe teased her.

"Liza, will you help me rewrap the presents after we eat?" Mandie asked.

"I sho' will, Missy," Liza replied as they continued into the dining room. "Jes' you give me time to git through dinner."

"I'll be in my room," Mandie told her.

"May I help?" Joe teased as they all sat down at the table.

"Of course not," Mandie said. "How about entertaining Hilda to keep her out of my room?"

"Me? Entertain Hilda?" Joe laughed. "That's impossible."

"You could at least try," Mandie said.

"All right," Joe finally agreed.

Hilda was across the table from them and probably couldn't hear their conversation, but she swayed slightly in her chair, humming to herself and repeating the word *secret* in a sing-song voice.

Eventually, dinner conversation turned to the question of how soon Elizabeth and the others would be able to get back.

Mr. Bond shook his head slowly. "Could be worse over there in those mountains around Tellico than it is here," he said. "Then again, it may not be as bad. We'll just have to wait and see."

Mandie looked straight at him. "Mother said in the message that they would be home in time for Christmas, and I know they will," she said firmly. "Besides"—she glanced around the table—"the surprise she has for me is for Christmas, and since none of y'all will tell me what it is, she'll have to be home in time to let me know what the surprise is."

No one answered her, and Mandie guessed that they

were all hoping Mandie's mother would come home soon and get the surprise business over with so they could have some peace.

During the lull in the conversation, Hilda hummed quietly to herself.

After the meal was over, Mandie reminded Joe to try to keep Hilda downstairs while she worked in her room. Joe said he would see if Hilda would like to play checkers by the fireplace in the parlor. Mandie wasn't sure how that would work, but she headed upstairs hopefully.

As she pulled the presents out of her trunk and laid them on the bed, she decided to get new paper to wrap them. Hurrying down the hallway to the sewing room, she hoped she wouldn't find the wrapping supplies in such a mess again.

But this time when she went into the sewing room, everything was in order. All the paper was neatly placed on a shelf along with the ribbons. The scissors were on the table. But when she looked for the plentiful red paper she had used before, she couldn't find even a scrap of it. She finally decided on a roll of white tissue paper, which they often used for wrapping gifts. Taking the whole roll, as well as the scissors and the ribbons, she hurried back to her room.

Liza came in just as she began to pull the old paper off one of the presents. Suddenly Mandie realized that it was the red scarf for Liza, and she quickly opened the trunk lid and dropped the scarf inside, hoping the girl didn't see it.

"Jes' tell me what you wants done, and I'll he'p," Liza said, sitting next to Mandie on the rug by the fire.

"All the presents on the bed there have to be re-wrapped with new paper," Mandie told her, stretching out the paper on the rug. "The old paper is too wrinkled. You know, I looked for some more of that red paper in the sewing room and there wasn't even a little piece of it anywhere."

"I knows." Liza clasped her hand to her mouth and didn't say another word.

"You know? You mean you knew there was none of it left?" Mandie asked.

"Dat's right, Missy. I knows it's all gone," Liza replied, watching as Mandie took a small present from the bed, tore the old wrapping off, and began rewrapping it in the new paper.

"Who in the world used all that paper?" Mandie asked, preoccupied with measuring a new piece. "There was a pile of it."

Liza ignored the question. "You cuts de paper and I he'p wrap up." She reached for the present and paper Mandie had in her hand. "I ain't much good at cuttin' straight."

"All right. You wrap and I'll cut," Mandie agreed.

It was a slow process because the girls took their time and talked a lot while they were wrapping. Mandie had to tell Liza who each present was for with the understanding that Liza would never tell anyone what they would be getting from Mandie for Christmas.

They were almost finished when Mandie heard horses on the road. She jumped up and ran to the window with Liza right behind. There was a two-horse wagon going by, but it seemed to have a hard time getting down the snow-covered road.

"It's not coming here," Mandie said in disappointment.

"No, but look, Missy. Look down there!" Liza pointed

excitedly toward the front porch below. They could see just a corner of it from where they were.

Mandie quickly saw where Liza was pointing. "There was Hilda on the front porch, walking backward down the front steps.

"What in de worl' is dat Hilda girl doin' now?" Liza asked.

"She's following the footprints we found. Look!" Mandie cried. "And I do believe she has some big shoes on her feet. Let's go see."

The girls rushed downstairs and didn't even stop for coats. They jerked open the front door in time to see Hilda walking backward across the front yard toward the summerhouse.

Mandie ran down to the walkway. "Hilda!" she yelled. "Come back here! Where are you going?"

Hilda paid no attention but kept going backward till she reached the summerhouse. Then she stepped up the stairs backward and went inside.

Mandie turned to Liza. "You're not wearing boots, and I'm not either. Will you stay here and see that she doesn't disappear while I run and get a coat and some boots? I'll be right back."

Mandie came into the house just as Joe came down the hallway toward the parlor.

"What's going on?" Joe asked.

Mandie reached into the closet under the stairs, trying to find a pair of boots. "Hilda is out there in the summerhouse. She walked backward all the way right in the track of the footprints. And I do believe she was wearing somebody else's big shoes."

"I'll go get her," Joe volunteered. He ran out the door.

Mandie followed and waited on the walkway while Joe

raced across the lawn to where Hilda was sitting in the summerhouse. She saw Joe take Hilda's hand, trying to get her to come back with him. But Hilda resisted.

"Hilda, I have a secret!" Mandie called to her.

"We got lotsa secrets!" yelled Liza.

Hilda got up and started back with Joe. Evidently the word *secret* worked magic. As the girl came out into the yard, Joe tried to help her walk in the snow, but Hilda pushed his hand away and carefully put her feet down in the big footprints in the snow. Slowly, she made her way back to the porch and then stopped and smiled as Mandie joined her. "Secret," Hilda said.

"Hilda, you have on some man's shoes," Mandie said, looking down at the girl's feet. "Where did you get them?"

"Secret," Hilda repeated, starting for the door.

Mandie laid a hand on the girl's arm. "You're the one who made those footprints before, aren't you? she asked. "You did it backward for some reason."

Hilda pulled away and stepped out of the shoes. Leaving them on the porch, she rushed inside the house.

Joe scratched his head. "I wonder where she got these," he said, picking up the shoes.

Mandie looked at them. "I do believe they're Uncle John's," she said. "He keeps a pair in the closet in the hallway to walk outside in bad weather. Let's look and see if his are in the closet."

Liza followed them inside where they searched the closet under the front stairs. John Shaw's shoes were not there.

"If dat don't beat all!" Liza exclaimed.

Mandie sighed. "I'll never understand why Hilda does the things she does."

"Nobody does," Joe replied.

Suddenly Mandie gasped. "The presents!" She ran for the stairway.

Liza followed, and Joe just stood there staring.

"Hilda may be in my room, getting into my presents," Mandie called back to Joe.

But when the girls opened the door to Mandie's room, Hilda was not there. Nothing had been disturbed.

Mandie breathed a sigh of relief. "Thank goodness," she said. "Let's get these things finished and put them under the tree."

The girls soon had all the presents wrapped again, and they carried them down to the parlor. No one was there. Carefully, they laid the gifts beneath the Christmas tree.

"I hope nothing happens to them again," Mandie said.

"Never can tell round dis place," Liza murmured.

"And I still have to find out where my green-wrapped presents went," Mandie reminded her. "I'm running out of time."

"Maybe they'll jes' come back like dese did," Liza told her.

"I hope so." Mandie sighed again.

Chapter 10 / Snowball and the Christmas Tree

Liza again woke Mandie the next morning. Hilda slept soundly at Mandie's side, and Snowball was curled up at the foot of the bed.

"Missy, Missy!" Liza said softly, laying her hand on Mandie's shoulder. "Time to git up. Today's Sunday and Miz Taft say ev'ybody goin' to church."

Mandie stretched and jumped out of bed, dumping Snowball onto the floor. She warmed herself in front of the fireplace, and Hilda opened one eye to see what was going on.

"It be past time to git up," Liza told Mandie. "Past time, 'cause somebody else done been up and put all dem green-wrapped presents back under de tree, and—"

"My presents are back?" Mandie interrupted. "Are they all right?"

Liza stirred up the fire to make it burn better. "I don't rightly be knowin'," she replied. "Dey all got messed-up paper, too, like dem other ones."

"Oh, no!" Mandie moaned, grabbing her robe and putting it on. "I have to go see."

"But de other ones, dey still there, too." Liza followed Mandie to the parlor with Snowball racing after them. But Hilda did not come.

Mandie ran over to the tree and knelt to look at her presents. Evidently, the green ones had been unwrapped and twisted back up in a mess.

Mandie sat on the floor and almost cried. "Why is somebody doing this to me? I don't understand who it can be."

Liza knelt beside Mandie and put her arm around her. "Missy, don't worry 'bout it too much. I'll he'p you wrap 'em all up agin in new paper," she said.

Mandie hugged her tightly. "Oh, Liza, I love you," she said tearfully. "You're always so good to me."

"I loves you, too, Missy. But now I gotta git in de kitchen and he'p 'bout breakfus'. Dat's what Mistuh John be payin' me fo'," Liza said, rising.

Mandie wiped her eyes with the sleeve of her robe. "You probably think I don't have anything for you for Christmas because you saw what was in all the red-wrapped presents," she said. "But I have something beautiful for you, and I had to hide it so you wouldn't see it. It's not down here with all the other presents."

"Dat's all right, Missy," Liza replied. "When you gives me yo' love, dat's enough." She started for the door. "Now I really gotta go or dat Aunt Lou, she be scoldin' me good. When you gits ready to wrap all dem things agin, jes' let me know, and I'll he'p."

"Thanks, Liza." Mandie followed her out of the parlor and turned to the stairway as Liza went on down the hallway to the kitchen.

"I wonder how much money Uncle John pays Liza," Mandie said to herself as she climbed the stairs. "My father used to say that good people were worth their weight in gold. I sure think Liza is."

Back in her room, Mandie noticed that Hilda was still in bed. She knew Hilda was awake, so she shook the girl's feet. "Come on, get up," she coaxed. "Today is Sunday and we're all going to church."

Hilda sat up in bed, and Mandie walked over to the window and drew the draperies to see outside.

"Come look, Hilda," Mandie said. "The weather is much better today. Look, the snow is melting into little streams and puddles. No wonder Grandmother expects us to go to church. The roads will be passable."

Hilda joined her at the window and looked out.

Mandie turned to the brown-haired girl suddenly. "Hilda, do you know who took my presents from under the tree?" she asked. "You remember, the red, green, red, green ones we put there."

"Red, green, red, green," Hilda repeated, smiling as she danced about. "Secret. Secret."

"Oh, well." Mandie gave up and started to get dressed.

"Hilda, I don't think you've been to our church before. We go to that big church across the road there. All my relatives on my father's side are buried there except my father. He's buried back at Charley Gap on top of a mountain. That's the land he loved."

Hilda gave another quick glance out the window, then walked back to the fireplace and began undressing. Mandie watched to see what Hilda would put on, but she didn't say a word.

Hilda picked up the dress she had worn the day before, the one with the buttons on the front. As Mandie watched, she put it on right and quickly buttoned it correctly, smiling at Mandie all the while.

"I know one thing, Hilda," Mandie said, putting on her own dress. "You sure like dresses that open in the front, don't you?"

Hilda only smiled. Putting on her stockings and slippers, she finished before Mandie and rushed out of the room.

When Mandie got down to breakfast, she expected to find Hilda there, but she was nowhere in sight. Only Mrs. Taft sat at the table.

Mandie picked up a plate and went to the sideboard. "Good morning, Grandmother," she said. "Hilda came down ahead of me, but she didn't come in here, did she?"

"No, I haven't seen her," Mrs. Taft replied, "but we'll have to keep her in sight today because we are all going to church."

Mandie brought her filled plate to the table and sat down beside her grandmother. "Guess what happened during the night?" Without waiting for an answer, she told her grandmother about the green presents reappearing under the tree, and she described the condition they were in.

"I still think it must be Hilda, dear," Mrs. Taft insisted. "I can't think of anyone else who would do such a thing."

"I don't know what to think anymore," Mandie admitted. "I don't think it could be Liza. She's so kind and sympathetic about it all."

"No, I wouldn't think Liza would do such a thing," Mrs. Taft agreed. She sipped her coffee. "Let's just keep this to ourselves for the time being. That way, maybe we'll catch the culprit."

"I'll only tell Joe. I'm sure he's not the one," Mandie said. "And of course Liza knows about it already."

Within a few minutes Mr. and Mrs. Burns, Jason Bond,

and Joe came into the room and served themselves some breakfast from the sideboard.

"Sure am glad to see all that snow beginnin' to melt away," Jake Burns said as they all sat at the table.

"Me, too," Mandie said. "And I'll be glad to get out and go to church today. It'll be a nice change from being shut up in the house."

Jason Bond offered to have the rig waiting for them at the back door. "Even though the church is just across the road, we'll drive you over so you ladies won't get your feet wet," he said.

"That's very thoughtful of you, Mr. Bond," Mrs. Taft replied. "We appreciate that."

Later, while everyone was rushing around to get ready, Hilda showed up at the breakfast table. No one had time to question her about where she had been. They knew they wouldn't get any answers anyway.

When they got to church, they found that the pastor had managed to get into town on horseback from his farm out in Macon County. The Sunday school classes put on their annual Christmas play, and the congregation joined in, singing Christmas carols.

Throughout the church service, Mandie watched Hilda, who sat next to her in the pew, and she wondered how much the girl understood.

Hilda just sat there smiling, her gaze fixed on what was happening in the front of the church. When the play had a Christmas tree in it with presents underneath, Hilda started her singsong, "Red, green, red, green."

Mrs. Taft, who sat on the other side of Hilda, tried to quiet her. She took Hilda's hand in hers and patted it.

Hilda smiled and hushed. But when everyone stood to sing some Christmas songs with the cast of the play and one song mentioned *presents*, Hilda began singing loudly, "Red, green, red, green." And she wouldn't stop until the carols were finished.

At the end of the service, the pastor stood at the door shaking hands. When he shook hands with Hilda, she smiled and said, "Red, green, red, green." The pastor looked perplexed, but he simply smiled and turned to the next ones in line.

Sunday dinner was cooked on Saturday in the Shaw household because all the servants were encouraged to go to church on Sunday. There was no work for anyone to do except warming up the food and putting it on the table. Everyone always pitched in and helped.

As soon as they got home that Sunday, Mandie quickly changed her clothes and ran to the kitchen to help Liza. And Joe soon joined them.

Mrs. Taft stuck her head in the kitchen doorway with the Burnses right behind her, but Aunt Lou shook a big spoon at them and ordered them away. "Now dis heah kitchen done be full, and we don't need de likes o' you folks. "Y'all don't know how to do anything the way we does it heah, anyhow. Jes' go sit down. Dinnuh be on de table in a minute."

"Well, if you say so, Aunt Lou," Mrs. Taft replied. "I thought since everyone was helping, I would see what I could do. But if you think the kitchen is too crowded, I will get out of the way." She turned to Mr. and Mrs. Burns. "Let's go sit at the table. It looks like the food will be served shortly."

When they had left and closed the door, Mandie whispered to Liza, "As soon as we eat, let's fix up those presents."

"We sho' will," Liza agreed.

When they were almost finished eating dinner, once again Mandie asked Joe to entertain Hilda so she and Liza could get the presents wrapped after dinner.

"You know I can't do anything with her," Joe objected. "If she wants to do something, I can't stop her. She just doesn't understand anything."

"You can try," Mandie said. "See if you can keep her attention away from me till I get the presents out from under the tree and take them to my room."

After they had been excused and Mandie started to leave the table, Joe turned to Hilda. "Come on, Hilda," he said. "I have a secret. Want to see?"

"Secret," Hilda repeated, following him out of the room.

Mandie watched them for a moment, wondering what Joe's newly invented secret would be.

Joe led Hilda to the back porch, where he picked up a piece of left-over mistletoe. "Look," he said mysteriously. "You hang this overhead like this"—he raised it above the doorway—"and then when someone walks under it, you grab them and kiss them. That's to show that you love them and wish them a Merry Christmas. Understand?"

Hilda just stood there, so Mandie hurried into the parlor to gather the messed-up presents.

Back in her room, Liza once more joined her and together they rewrapped the presents in the new white tissue paper from the sewing room.

"Now my presents will all look alike," Mandie said as they cut paper, wrapped the gifts, and tied ribbons. "But I guess that's all right."

Liza surveyed their work. "Dis heah paper prettier den de other paper anyway," she said.

Mandie stood. "Now we have to get them back down under the tree," she said, bending to pick up an armful.

Liza took the rest, and the two girls went back down to the parlor. Mrs. Taft was sitting by the fireplace, reading her Bible. But no one else was around.

"We've got them all wrapped again," Mandie told her grandmother as they scattered them among the other presents under the tree.

"They look pretty, dear," Mrs. Taft said. "I'll bring mine down tonight, I suppose, and add them to the pile. I noticed there are several others there besides yours—with no names, of course. All this present business has got to be a big secret." She laughed.

"That's what Hilda thinks," Mandie replied. "Where is everybody?"

"Mr. Bond is out in back, helping the Burnses get their horse and wagon ready to go home," Mrs. Taft told her.

But at that moment Mrs. Burns came into the room with a disappointed look on her face. She sat down by the fireplace. "Well, looks like y'all gonna hafta put up with us one more night," she said. "That horse seems to have throwed a shoe, and you know the smithy ain't open on Sunday."

"I'm sorry about the horse, Ludie," Mrs. Taft said, "but we will be delighted to have y'all for another night."

"We shore are wearin' our welcome out, but I reckon it cain't be helped this time," Ludie Burns replied.

Mandie smiled at the woman. "I'm glad y'all are staying till tomorrow because my mother will be home then. Besides, it will be Christmas Eve, and we'll have a big dinner."

"Bless you, little lady," Mrs. Burns replied. "But to be honest with you, I'd much rather be in my own home for

Christmas Eve. We have so much that needs to be done there."

Suddenly a streak of white bounced in from the hallway, and everyone watched in dismay as Snowball ran directly to the Christmas tree, jumped in among the presents, and climbed his way to the top of the tall pine. There he stopped and meowed for someone to get him down.

Mandie jumped up and put her hands on her hips. "Snowball," she reprimanded the kitten, "I don't know how in the world anyone is going to get you down without turning the tree over, you silly cat!"

A voice behind Mandie spoke up. "I'll git a ladder and git him down for you, Missy."

Mandie turned to find Jake Burns standing inside the doorway.

"Do you think it's possible?" Mandie asked. "That tree is twelve feet tall, remember?"

"I think I can reach him from a ladder all right," Jake said, leaving the room.

Then Joe and Hilda came into the parlor. Joe shrugged, indicating that he had given up on Hilda.

"We're all done anyway, Joe," Mandie assured him.

Snowball swayed slightly at the top of the tree and let out an angry hiss, baring his teeth.

Joe looked up and saw Snowball. "That crazy cat!"

"Mr. Burns has gone for a ladder to get him down," Mandie told him.

Jake returned with Mr. Bond and a ladder. The two men set it up as near the tree as they could get.

"I'll go up if you'll hold the ladder down here," Jake said to Jason Bond.

Joe walked over to help hold it steady as Mr. Burns

climbed toward the top of the tree. As he reached for the kitten, Snowball snarled angrily at the man and backed away out of Jake's reach.

Hilda suddenly seemed bored with the cat in the tree and stooped to look at the presents underneath. "Red, green, red, green," she sang.

At that instant Snowball lost his grip and began falling down through the limbs of the tree, snatching at things with his claws as he went. He landed on Hilda's back.

Hilda screamed and straightened up. And Snowball ran out of the room.

Mrs. Taft examined Hilda's back and found that Snowball had not scratched her. But the tree was a mess. The ornaments were knocked out of place and the garlands were tangled along the path Snowball had fallen.

Mandie stood there, blinking back the tears. "Sometimes I think I might just give that cat away," she cried.

Liza, who had been standing in the doorway, watching, hurried forward to put her arm around Mandie. "Now, Missy, you know you don't mean dat," she said. "You know you loves dat kitten so much you wouldn't take a thousand dollars fo' him."

"I don't know," Mandie said.

"I know," Joe spoke up. "Like I always say, that's a dumb cat. He just didn't know any better, so you have to forgive him. Come on, let's get the tree decorations straightened."

Mandie just looked at him for a moment; then without a word she joined him and Liza in repairing the damage Snowball had done to the tree.

Hilda stayed close to Mrs. Taft and watched.

Mandie picked up a silver ball that had rolled across the rug. "I'll be glad when Christmas finally comes before the tree and the presents all get destroyed," she said.

"Tomorrow is Christmas Eve," Joe said, trying to comfort her, "and our parents will be home then. You can count on that for sure."

Mandie gave a sigh, then brightened as she helped with the tree. Her mother would be home tomorrow. She had missed her, and it would be so good to see her—then, too, she would *finally* know what the big surprise was.

Chapter 11 / Trapped!

Mandie awakened early on Christmas Eve morning. Throwing back the heavy quilts, she jumped out of bed. Liza had apparently built the fire in the fireplace already but hadn't bothered to wake her.

Hilda was still sleeping, and Mandie playfully pulled the covers off the girl and tickled her feet. "Get up, Hilda," Mandie cried. "It's Christmas Eve."

Hilda, startled awake, withdrew her ticklish feet from Mandie's reach and then kicked hard, sending Mandie flying backward onto the floor.

Mandie got up, laughing. "I guess that pays me back," she said. "Come on, let's get dressed and go downstairs. Today is Christmas Eve and tomorrow is Christmas. My mother and Uncle John and Joe's parents will be home today for certain."

Hilda just lay there, listening and watching Mandie as she moved about, finding a dress and stockings to put on.

Mandie reached into the chifferobe and pulled out a bright red dress that buttoned all the way down the front. She held it up for Hilda to see. "Look at what I've got,"

Mandie said, trying to entice her to get out of bed.

Hilda jumped up and snatched the dress from Mandie's hand.

Mandie laughed. "That worked, didn't it? You can wear my red dress, Hilda. I know you like it because it buttons down the front. Let me help you put it on."

Hilda backed away from Mandie into the far corner. She dropped the red dress onto the rug behind her and didn't take her eyes off Mandie. Hastily taking off her nightgown, she put on a petticoat she had left hanging on a chair the night before. Then she unbuttoned the front of the red dress and slipped into it. Quickly buttoning the buttons, she mismatched them, so the dress hung lopsided.

"Hilda, you've got it buttoned wrong," Mandie said, advancing toward her. "Let me rebutton it for you. Please?"

Hilda violently shook her head, her long brown hair swirling about; then she sat on the rug to put on her stockings and slippers.

Mandie gave up and hastily dressed herself. This was going to be a happy day. She would finally get to see her mother. Brushing her long blonde hair, she tied it back with a blue ribbon to match the blue dress she was wearing.

Hilda watched her, and when Mandie laid the brush down, Hilda snatched it up and began brushing her hair.

Mandie quickly rummaged through a dresser drawer and came up with a bright red ribbon to match the dress Hilda had on. She held it out to the girl.

Hilda slowly took it and looked it over, evidently not knowing how to put it in her hair.

"I'll tie your hair back with it like mine," Mandie said,

picking up the brush where Hilda had laid it down.

Hilda stood still and waited to see what Mandie was going to do. Mandie led her over in front of the mirror so she could watch.

"You do it like this," Mandie told her as she pulled the brown hair back, looped the ribbon around it, and tied a bow. "Pretty."

Hilda gazed at herself in the mirror and then looked up at Mandie with a smile. "Pretty," she said.

The little ceramic clock on the mantelpiece began to chime.

"Oh goodness, it's only seven o'clock," Mandie said. She ran across the room to pull back the draperies.

The first streaks of sunrise were just beginning to show through the dark sky.

"Thank goodness, it's going to be a clear day," Mandie said to herself. "Let's go eat, Hilda."

"Eat," Hilda repeated. She smiled and followed Mandie down the stairs to the breakfast room.

When they got there, Joe was the only one at the table, and he had a plate heaped with food in front of him. He greeted the girls happily. "It's going to be a great day!" he said.

Mandie smiled at him. It took a lot to get Joe excited about anything. He must have really missed his parents.

After helping Hilda fill a plate and fixing one for herself, Mandie sat down next to Joe with Hilda on her other side. "And tomorrow will be even better!" she exclaimed.

"That's right," Joe agreed. "So much has happened this year that it's hard to believe."

"I know. First my father . . . died . . ." She still had trouble saying the word sometimes. "Then I came to live with Uncle John, whom I didn't even know until Uncle Ned

136

told me about him. Then Uncle John sent for my mother from over in Asheville, and I met her for the first time. And then after Uncle John married my mother, I was sent away to boarding school in Asheville, and now here I am back in Franklin for Christmas." She sighed deeply.

"And your mother was so thrilled to find you at last and to know you were actually alive," Joe added. "I can't imagine being separated from my parents."

"Come to think of it, Hilda is separated from her parents, too, but for a good reason," Mandie said as she cut into a piece of ham. "Remember? They kept her locked in a room because she can't talk hardly at all. And when she ran away and hid in our school attic, and Celia and I found her, they gave her to my grandmother. Can you imagine giving away your child?"

"Never!" Joe replied, emphatically hitting his fist on the table.

Hilda jumped.

"I'm sorry, Hilda," Joe apologized. "I didn't mean to scare you."

Hilda smiled, and after eating another bite of her breakfast, she began her singsong again. "Red, green, red, green. Secret."

When Liza came into the room with a pot of hot coffee, she didn't speak as she filled Mandie's cup.

Mandie noticed that the young maid didn't seem very happy. "Good morning, Liza," she said.

"Mawnin', Missy," Liza murmured, filling Joe's cup.

"You must not have been the one who built the fire in my room this morning because no one woke me up," Mandie reasoned.

"I built de fire, Missy," Liza said hesitantly. "I jes' thought I'd better let you sleep."

Mandie looked at her sharply. "Why did you want to let me sleep? It's Christmas Eve day, and my mother is coming home today!"

"I knows dat, Missy," Liza replied, pausing with the pot of coffee still in her hand. "I jes' didn't want to—"

"To what?" Mandie asked quickly. "Is something wrong?"

Liza simply nodded.

Mandie jumped up. "No, not again!" she exclaimed.

Liza nodded again, and Mandie ran into the parlor with Joe close behind. They looked at the Christmas tree, and every one of Mandie's presents was gone. The other presents were all there, but not Mandie's.

Mandie plopped down on the floor by the tree and cried.

Joe sat beside her and patted her hand. "Don't cry, Mandie. We'll find them," he assured her.

"I don't know how," Mandie sobbed. "We haven't been able to find any of them yet when they disappeared."

"Somebody must really be heartless to keep doing this," Joe said. "Come on. Let's start looking."

Liza stood at the parlor door. "Want me to he'p?" she offered.

"Thank you, Liza," Mandie said through her tears, "but Aunt Lou would want to know what you're doing, and we don't want anyone else to know about the missing presents until we find out who's taking them."

"If I kin he'p, jes' you let me know, Missy," Liza said as she left the room.

Joe stood and helped Mandie up. "Let's get started," he said.

Listlessly, Mandie followed Joe around the house as they poked into every room and every hiding place they could think of. The library was the last room on their search upstairs.

As Mandie pushed open the door to the library, she looked up at the portrait of her Cherokee grandmother. "Joe," she said, "if you don't mind, I think I'll stay in here a few minutes to think. Why don't you go back downstairs and see what Hilda is doing?"

"I understand," Joe replied, turning to go down the hallway. "I'll see you when you come back downstairs."

Mandie went on into the library and closed the door. There were shelves on three sides of the room, running over with books. Uncle John's desk stood in front of a large stained-glass window, and on the opposite side of the room was an elaborate couch. On either side of her grandmother's picture over the mantelpiece, there were sconces on the wall, holding candles. But the draperies were open, and the sun was shining brightly, so there was no need to light them.

Mandie roamed around the room, stopping to stare at the portrait of her father's mother. Her grandmother had been a full-blooded Cherokee, and her great-grandfather had built a secret tunnel into this very house to hide the girl and her Indian family from the white men who were moving them all out of the territory in 1838. Mandie knew the story well now. She stood there studying the face of the young girl in the portrait and wondered what it would have been like to have her Cherokee grandmother alive now.

Mandie wandered over to the small door hidden behind a curtain in one corner. She pulled the curtain back and pushed on the door. To her surprise the door was not locked. She stepped inside the opening, which months earlier she had discovered was the entrance to the secret tunnel. Immediately the door swung shut! Fumbling in the dark, she realized there was no door handle on this side, and the latch had clicked shut.

Mandie's heart beat rapidly. It was dark in the tunnel, and she knew no one was anywhere near to let her out. She beat on the door a few times, then gave up. She would just have to make her way through the darkness down to the tunnel's exit in the woods behind the house. Then another thought worried her. *What if that's closed shut with snow, too?*

"I'll just have to go and see," she said to herself, feeling her way down the many steps.

Soon she heard a scurrying sound around her feet and realized it must be mice. Breathlessly, she continued on, stomping her feet to keep the mice away from her.

As she got nearer the other end of the tunnel, suddenly there was a loud crash. She stopped and took a deep breath. Then she started quoting her favorite Bible verse, "What time I am afraid I will put my trust in thee." She stood perfectly still for a few moments, holding her breath and listening. There was no other sound, so she hurried on.

"The outside door must be near now," she told herself. But at that moment she stumbled into something that shuffled around her feet and legs.

She gasped with fright. In her mind she was saying, *I told God I would trust in Him, and look what I'm doing.* Squaring her shoulders, she stepped forward and ran head-on into the outside door of the tunnel. Breathing a sigh of relief, she felt around for the key to the outside door. It always hung on a nail nearby. She found the nail, but there was no key.

Mandie pounded on the door. "Somebody come and

let me out!" she cried loudly.

But after there was no response, she finally gave up and sat down to rest in the darkness. As she sat, she felt something soft under her and began exploring. There seemed to be several different objects on the floor near her.

She got excited as she picked the things up and examined them with her fingers. "My presents!" She gasped, hugging them all close to her. "How did they get here?"

At intervals, she would get up and pound on the door with her fists; but when no one came, she would sit down again among her presents. It seemed she had been there for hours when a vague gleam of light appeared up the stairs behind her. She jumped up and squinted up the steps.

The light became a little brighter. Then a voice called her name.

"Joe! I'm down here," she called excitedly as she made out his form in the light of the lamp he was carrying.

"Mandie, what on earth are you doing down here?" he asked, coming down the steps. As he got closer, he saw the scattered packages. "Don't tell me. Your presents!"

"Oh, Joe, the door shut on me up in the library, and I couldn't get back out," Mandie explained, trembling. "And the key for this door is missing. And then I found my presents all over the floor."

"When you didn't come back for so long I went up to the library to look for you," Joe said. "You weren't there, but when I saw the curtain pulled back to the door of the tunnel, I came looking." He set the lamp down on the floor to help her pick up presents.

"I'm so thankful you did," Mandie said, trying to balance her armload. "I must have been in here for hours."

When the two of them had picked everything up, Joe took the lamp to lead the way back upstairs into the house. "Oh, I forgot to tell you why I came looking for you," he said. "Our parents are back, and—"

Mandie didn't hear another word. She raced ahead of Joe up the steps and arrived at the top, out of breath. "Wait a minute," she said. "How are we going to get back out?"

Joe stepped ahead of her. "Don't worry," he said. "I turned the latch back so it wouldn't lock."

"Whew!" Mandie said, pushing through the door. Inside the library, she dropped all her presents on the floor and hurried downstairs, with Joe right behind.

In the parlor, Elizabeth Shaw, Mandie's beautiful blonde mother, was sitting on the settee next to Uncle John.

Mandie rushed to embrace her mother and then turned to hug her stepfather. "I'm so glad to see y'all," she said, dropping onto a footstool in front of them. "I thought you'd never get home."

Joe happily greeted his mother and father, who were sitting by the fire with Mrs. Taft. Then he sat nearby in an empty chair by the window.

Mandie gave her mother and Uncle John a somewhat jumbled account of what had been going on since she had come home from school for the holidays. Then she leaned back against her mother and said, "I'm so thankful you got home in time for Christmas. It's my very first Christmas with you, Mother," she reminded her.

"I know, dear," Elizabeth said, stroking her daughter's

blonde hair. "That's why we made sure we got here before tomorrow."

Uncle John patted Mandie on the shoulder. "We had to go on horseback a little ways, and then we got the train," he explained. "Fortunately, we made it on time to meet the train's schedule."

Mandie looked back at them. "I'm sorry that your friend died," she said. "Couldn't Dr. Woodard doctor him and get him well?"

Dr. Woodard sat forward. "He was pretty old, Amanda," he said, "and in bad health."

"In fact," Uncle John added, "he was so old that he knew my father when my father was young."

"I wish I could have known him if he knew my grand-father," Mandie said wistfully.

There was a lull in the conversation for a moment, and finally Elizabeth got up from the settee. "I'm tired after the long trip, dear," she said to Mandie. "I have to go lie down awhile."

"May I go upstairs with you, Mother?" Mandie asked, standing up.

"Let me rest awhile first, please," Elizabeth replied. "I'll be back down for dinner, and then we'll talk some more."

Mandie gave her mother a tight hug. "Please hurry back down," she said.

Uncle John walked over and put his arm around Elizabeth as they both headed for the stairs.

Mandie ran over to him and looked up into his eyes. "Are you going, too, Uncle John?" she protested.

"I'm a little worn out, too," he said, giving her a hug. "But I promise we won't rest too long."

Dr. and Mrs. Woodard rose and started to leave the

room, too. Mandie could tell Joe didn't want his parents to leave, either, but he didn't say anything.

"We'll all be back down for the noon meal," Dr. Woodard assured them.

After they left the room, Mandie turned to Joe. "I wonder where the Burnses are. And Mr. Bond," she said.

"Mr. and Mrs. Burns went home," Joe replied. "And Jason Bond is tending to the horses in the barn."

"I just remembered. The presents!" Mandie exclaimed. "I have to see what kind of shape they're in this time. Come on." Mandie led the way back to the library where she had dropped them on the floor.

As they picked up each one and examined it, they found that the wrapping paper had not been disturbed.

"Thank goodness I don't have to wrap them again," Mandie said. "Will you help me put them back under the Christmas tree?"

"Mandie, I don't think I'd do that if I were you," Joe cautioned. "Every time you put anything under the tree, it disappears. Why don't you lock them in your trunk or somewhere until tomorrow morning when we exchange gifts?"

Mandie thought for a minute. "You're right, Joe," she agreed. "Let's take them to my room."

With her presents safely stored away, Mandie felt relieved. Her mother and Uncle John were home, and when her mother came back downstairs, Mandie would find out what the surprise was.

Later that afternoon as she sat alone with her mother near the fireplace in the sun room, she eagerly asked about the surprise, but her mother refused to tell her.

"I said the surprise is for Christmas," Elizabeth said, smiling at her daughter. "Tomorrow is Christmas Day. I'll tell you then."

"Mother, please?" Mandie begged. "I've been waiting all this time to find out what it is, and everybody else seems to know, but they won't say. Please tell me."

"No, dear," her mother insisted. "We'll save it for to-morrow morning, Christmas Day."

That night after a special supper, Christmas carolers came by, and the family all joined in the singing. And later there was hot cocoa, coffee, and cookies in the parlor by the Christmas tree. Lots of other presents had mysteri-ously appeared beneath the tree by then.

But through all the festivities, it was hard for Mandie to join in the Christmas spirit.

When she went to bed, she tossed and turned, wishing she could sleep the night away so she could find out what the surprise was. Finally she fell asleep, trying to figure it all out.

Chapter 12 / The Big Surprise!

" 'For unto you is born this day in the city of David a Saviour, which is Christ the Lord. . . .' " Uncle John read from the second chapter of Luke as they were all gathered in the parlor Christmas morning.

The servants were all present, and after the Bible reading, Uncle John handed out their pay raises and thanked them for a year of hard work. Then presents were exchanged. Mandie had brought hers back downstairs earlier that morning, adding them to the pile under the tree.

Each person gave everyone else some little something for Christmas, so the gift-giving took a lot of time. There were many ohs and ahs of pleasure as the gifts were unwrapped.

When the last one was handed out, Aunt Lou stepped forward to address Elizabeth. "We folks have a big present fo' you and Mistuh John, but we has to give it to you later," she said.

"Thank you, Aunt Lou," Elizabeth replied, "but I hope you didn't go to a lot of trouble and expense."

"No, ma'am, we made it all," the old housekeeper

assured her. She turned back to the other servants. "It's time fo' some breakfus'," she said. "Git goin' now."

As the servants left the room, Mandie sat on the rug fingering the sand-dollar necklace Tommy Patton had given her. Finally she pulled the paper off the present from her mother and Uncle John, revealing a complete set of encyclopedias. She gasped in delight. "Oh, thank you, Mother and Uncle John. I'll read every one of these."

John and Elizabeth laughed.

"That's exactly what we thought you'd do," Elizabeth teased. "You are always so curious about everything. You'll find the answers to many, many things in those books."

"Is this what the big surprise was?" Mandie asked, somewhat disappointed.

Elizabeth stood. "No, there's more," she said. "Now that all of us have opened our presents, let's get on into the breakfast room and eat. Then Mandie, you and I will have our little private session, dear."

Mandie could hardly eat a bite. She had received so many nice gifts, and now she was eager to know what her mother's big surprise was.

Finally, after breakfast, Mandie joined her mother in the sun room. She sat down next to her on the settee by the window, holding her breath in anticipation.

"Amanda, dear, I have a wonderful surprise for you," Elizabeth began, putting an arm around her daughter. "Since I have never discussed this kind of thing with you before, it's hard for me to find the right words." She paused.

Mandie sat still, her heart doing flip-flops inside.

"I suppose there's only one way to say this," Elizabeth began again. She looked directly into her daughter's blue eyes, so much like her own, and said, "God is sending you a little brother or sister. We won't know which until it gets here around June." She stopped, watching for Mandie's reaction.

Mandie thought she would smother to death with shock, anger ... She didn't know how to describe what she felt. She couldn't even speak, she was so overcome.

Elizabeth smiled brightly. "Now, isn't that a wonderful surprise?" she asked, stroking Mandie's blonde hair.

Mandie quickly jerked away. "It can't be my brother or sister because it doesn't belong to my daddy," she said, trembling. "It's my cousin because Uncle John is its father. That's what it is!"

Elizabeth tried to hold her close again, but she pulled away and jumped up.

"Amanda, I know this is something unexpected, but it's also something that is definitely going to happen," she said sternly. "So you might as well get used to the idea."

"I won't! I won't!" Mandie cried. Rushing out of the room, she ran blindly up the stairs and into her room, where she fell across the bed, sobbing wildly.

She was not going to share her mother with another boy or girl. No, she was not! She had finally found her real mother this year, and she was going to hold on to her. No one else was going to have a claim on her, not the least bit.

She cried until she could cry no more. Then she got up and sat by the window. Her eyes were so swollen, she could hardly see.

A long time later there was a gentle tap on her door. Ignoring it at first, she finally yelled, "Go away! I don't want to see anybody, whoever you are."

The door slowly opened a small crack, and Mandie looked up to see her father's old Cherokee friend, Uncle Ned, peeping through the doorway at her.

Mandie jumped up and ran to him. Flinging the door open, she hugged his neck. "Uncle Ned! Uncle Ned! I'm so glad to see you!" she cried. She took his hand and led him over to the windowseat. "Sit down, Uncle Ned."

The old Indian sat beside her and finally spoke. "Good to see Papoose," he said. "Sallie and Morning Star come, too."

"They did?" Mandie started to get up.

Uncle Ned grabbed her hand. "Wait, Papoose. First we talk."

Mandie reluctantly sat back down and realized instantly that her mother must have told him what had happened. "I know what you're going to say, Uncle Ned, but I'm not going to listen to you," she said angrily. "I don't want a brother or sister, and I'm not going to have one!"

"Papoose!" Uncle Ned spoke sharply as he held her hand. "Do not speak like that! God will hear you. God sends your mother this new papoose. He gives her great joy. You must have great joy, too. Must love new papoose."

"No, Uncle Ned, I won't!" Mandie remained stubborn.

"I never see Papoose make fuss like this," Uncle Ned said, a frown deepening the wrinkles in his weathered face. "Remember. Jim Shaw tell me watch over Papoose when he go to happy hunting ground. I watch. I not like what Papoose do now. Jim Shaw not like what Papoose do now."

"Leave my father out of this," Mandie said belligerently. "This has nothing to do with my father."

"Papoose wrong," Uncle Ned said. "Jim Shaw would

want wife Elizabeth happy. She happy now with John Shaw. They both happy now with new papoose coming. Big papoose make mother sad when jealous."

"Me jealous, Uncle Ned? Oh, no, I'm not." Mandie tried to pull her hand loose. "Uncle Ned, I really love you, and I don't want to hurt you, but let's not talk anymore about this. I don't want to hear about it."

"That will not make new papoose go away," the old Indian said. "Papoose be here in June. Must be loved."

"I will not love it, and there's nothing anyone can do about that," Mandie insisted. "Now if you don't mind, I'd like to go downstairs and see Sallie and Morning Star."

Uncle Ned released her hand and stood up. "Papoose look in mirror. Wash face first." He smiled and left the room.

Mandie quickly looked in the mirror and saw what he meant. Her eyes were red and swollen, and her hair was a mess. She hurried to the bathroom and washed her face in cold water. Then she came back and brushed out her long hair. Squaring her shoulders, she headed downstairs to see her friends. She hated to think of facing her mother again, but she couldn't stay in her room forever. So she walked slowly down the stairs.

Looking over the bannister, she saw Uncle Ned's granddaughter in the hallway below. "Sallie!" she cried excitedly. She rushed down and embraced her young Indian friend.

Sallie greeted her and smiled, but Mandie could tell something was wrong. She decided Sallie must know about the disagreement Mandie had with her mother.

Glancing into the parlor, Mandie saw all the adults in there, and she took Sallie aside. "Let's go back here and talk," she said, leading the way into the sun room. But when they got there, Mandie was surprised to see Joe sitting alone, looking out the window.

"Why are you here by yourself, Joe?" Mandie asked. Her voice sounded scratchy from all the crying she had done, and she tried not to look him straight in the face because of her swollen eyes.

"I know what happened between you and your mother, Mandie, and I figured you'd be coming back here instead of where your mother is in the parlor," he said as the two girls took seats nearby. "You see, if you remember, I told you that you wouldn't like the big surprise."

"Joe Woodard!" Mandie exclaimed. "Would you stop trying to read my mind?"

"You've got to admit, I do a pretty good job of it most of the time, don't I?" he said, laughing.

"I don't want to talk about it," Mandie said quickly. "Let's go outside for some fresh air, Sallie. "You, too, Joe, if you want to."

"That would be nice," Sally agreed.

Without another word the three got their coats from the hall tree and went out the front door. The snow had melted a lot more, and they wandered across the yard toward the summerhouse.

Suddenly Mandie stopped and pointed. "Isn't that Hilda out there?"

The three of them hurried in that direction. Hilda evidently didn't hear them coming, and when they stopped by the railing, she was sitting on the circular seat in the summerhouse, moving pieces of red and green paper around and singing, "Red, green, red, green, secret."

Mandie let out a moan. "Look! She has pieces of paper from my presents. It *was* her, after all. Remember how we caught her walking backward out here in the snow?"

Hilda heard them then and quickly tried to hide the pieces of paper as the three young people came near her. She dodged past them and ran back toward the big house. As she did she dropped the key to the tunnel door.

"Well, there's the solution to that mystery," Joe said, picking up the key.

"Let's see where she goes," Mandie said, hurrying after her. Joe and Sallie followed.

Hilda ran into the parlor and sat down next to Mrs. Taft, hiding the pieces of paper in the folds of her skirt. Mandie and Joe stopped in the doorway.

Morning Star, sitting by the fire, saw Mandie and came to hug her tight.

"Christmas merry," the old Indian squaw said the greeting backwards.

"Merry Christmas, Morning Star," Mandie said, giving her a hug. "I'm so glad you came to see us."

At that moment Abraham came to the parlor door, carrying the huge box Mandie and Joe had found in the attic.

The other servants followed Abraham into the room as he walked over and set the box down in front of Elizabeth.

"Come on, let's go back to the sun room," Joe urged Mandie and Sallie.

"Wait. I want to see what he's got in that box," Mandie said.

"Merry Christmas, Miz 'Lizbeth," Abraham said. "From all of us."

Elizabeth looked down at the big box. "Oh, Abraham, how nice," she replied. "Would you do me the honor of opening the box for me, please?" "Yessum," Abraham agreed. Within seconds he had opened the box, revealing a beautiful handmade cradle loaded with dainty hand-sewn baby clothes.

Excitedly, Elizabeth examined everything, showing each little garment to John.

Mandie turned and ran from the parlor to the sun room. Joe and Sallie joined her a few seconds later, and they all sat there quietly for a few minutes.

Finally Joe spoke. "Mandie, this is something you've got to learn to live with. It's not going to go away."

"No!" Mandie said emphatically.

"I wish I had a little brother or sister," Sallie said gently. "I would be so happy."

"Me, too," Joe added. "I always wanted a brother or sister to play with as I grew up."

Mandie looked doubtfully from one to the other. "But I don't want one. My mother sends me away to school, and now the new one will be allowed to stay home with her all the time. It's not fair."

"For goodness sakes, Mandie!" Joe exclaimed. "Think how you'll feel when you grow up and have children and the first one is jealous because the second one is coming along."

"Let's talk about something else," Mandie said.

Joe and Sallie looked at each other and changed the subject, but Mandie knew the situation wouldn't go away.

Christmas Day passed, and Mandie would not discuss the new baby with anyone. She was ashamed of the way she had acted, but she couldn't talk to her mother about it. And Elizabeth did not mention it again. She only looked at Mandie with sad eyes every time she saw her. Mandie completely ignored Uncle Ned, and he acted hurt. Finally everyone gave up talking to her about it.

Soon it was New Year's Eve, and Celia Hamilton and

her mother arrived. But Mandie wouldn't even talk to Celia about the baby.

That afternoon Celia, Mandie, Joe, and Sallie were all in the sun room, making various New Year's resolutions when Uncle Ned joined them.

He sat down next to Mandie. "Papoose, I read Big Book," he said, reaching for Mandie's hand. "I find verse. It say, little papooses love not in word or by tongue but in deed and in truth."

Mandie didn't say a word.

Joe sat forward. "I know exactly what you read, Uncle Ned." He grinned. "First John 3:18 says, 'My little children, let us not love in word, neither in tongue; but in deed and in truth.' Isn't that it?"

"Good boy." Uncle Ned nodded. He turned back to Mandie. "Papoose must do what Big Book say if Papoose want to see father in happy hunting ground some day."

Tears came to Mandie's eyes and she took a deep breath. "I'm sorry I talked to you like that, Uncle Ned," she apologized. "Please forgive me. I do love you."

"I love Papoose," Uncle Ned reminded her. "I forgive. But Papoose must ask mother forgive, too. Remember, Big Book say not let sun go down on anger."

Mandie sat silently for a moment. She looked at her three friends and then back to the old Indian. She *was* sorry. "All right, Uncle Ned," she finally relented. "I'll go tell Mother I'm sorry."

Mandie quickly left the room and found her mother all alone on the settee in the parlor. Walking up to face her, Mandie quickly said, "Mother, I'm sorry for the way I've acted about your baby. I'm really sorry. Please forgive me." She fell sobbing into her mother's open arms.

"I knew you didn't really mean what you said, dear. It

was just a shock to you, I know," Elizabeth said, cradling Mandie's head on her shoulder. "But the good Lord has seen fit to send us a baby, and we should be thrilled to have it." She patted the settee beside her, and Mandie sat down. "I know about that terrible stepsister you had when your father married that woman over there in Swain County," Elizabeth said. "I know how that woman was cruel to you and made such a difference between you and her own daughter."

Mandie looked up at her questioningly. "How do you know all these things?"

"Dr. Woodard told me a long time ago," Elizabeth replied. "But you see, Mandie, your Uncle John won't make any difference between you and the new baby. You love him and he loves you, and he will still love you just as much as he always has." She brushed a strand of Mandie's hair out of her eyes. "And of course no one could ever replace you in my heart. You will always have my love. I will just have to share it with the new baby, which is what you'll have to do."

Mandie dried her eyes. "Do you think it'll be a boy or a girl?" she asked, suddenly finding herself interested in this new little person.

"I have no idea, dear," Elizabeth replied.

"I hope it's a boy," Mandie said with a smile. "Then I'll still be the only girl."

"Whatever it is, we have to remember it was God's choice," Elizabeth reminded her. "Now, go back to your friends. I've got some things I need to do right now, such as talking to *my* mother."

Mandie hurried back to the sun room, and Uncle Ned was still there with the others, waiting to see what she had to say.

"Everything is all right now," Mandie told him. "Thank you."

Uncle Ned smiled as he rose and patted her head. "New papoose will be boy," he predicted.

Mandie looked up quickly. "But you don't really know..." she said. "That's what I want, too, though. A brother."

Everyone laughed, and the tension was broken. Mandie's anger had melted away.

The new year came in with a happy note. Everyone stayed up for midnight, including the servants. A midnight feast had been laid out on the dining room table for everyone to help themselves.

As the grandfather clock in the front hallway struck twelve, everyone called Happy New Year to each other.

All of a sudden Hilda burst into the room out of nowhere, dangling a big piece of mistletoe high over her head. She ran over to Mrs. Taft and gave her a little kiss on the cheek. "Love," she said. "Secret."

Everyone laughed, but Mandie and Joe laughed the loudest, realizing that Hilda had understood more than he thought when he told her he had a secret and showed her what to do with mistletoe.

Later, as the young people stood around, eating snacks, Mandie gave a little sigh. "I'm so glad I can start out the year 1901 with a clear conscience," she said. "I think it would be terrible to not be speaking to my mother."

"You should be thankful you have a mother, Mandie," Sallie said. "Remember, mine died a long time ago."

"I know," Mandie admitted. "I am thankful for so many things. God has been so wonderful to me this past year."

"But we've had our share of trials, too, haven't we, Mandie?" Celia added. "Like with April Snow at school? I sure hope that mouse is gone when we get back." She shivered.

"And I guess we still have another mystery to solve at school. Remember, we never did find out how April got into that play or why she didn't come back with the rest of us."

The next morning, on New Year's Day, they all slept longer than usual because they had stayed up so late. And after a leisurely breakfast, they were all gathered in the parlor.

Suddenly there was a knock on the front door. Liza went to answer it, and the parlor conversation hushed as everyone listened.

"Yessir, dey's a Missy 'Manda Shaw here in dis here house," Liza said, in the hallway.

"Could I see her, please?" a man's voice asked.

"Why sho'. Jes' you come on in. Dey's all in here." Soon she appeared in the doorway of the parlor with a tall, handsome man behind her. "Missy," she called across the room to Mandie, "dis here man wants to see you 'bout sumthin'." She stepped aside to let the man enter the parlor.

Mandie hurried across the room, looking the man over. He was not anyone she knew. But she had never seen such fine clothes before, nor such a nice-looking man.

The others remained silent, listening and watching.

"Are you Miss Amanda Shaw?" the man asked in an unusual accent.

"Yes sir, I'm Amanda Shaw," Mandie said.

The man removed a cream-colored envelope from his pocket and extended it to her. "Miss Amanda Shaw, greetings from the President of the United States, William McKinley, twenty-fifth president."

Mandie was speechless. Then she laughed. "You are joking!" She still didn't take the envelope, and everyone in the room waited.

"No, ma'am. I am very serious about this," the man replied. "Now if you will accept this envelope, I will be on my way."

Mandie smiled and slowly reached for the envelope. After the man gave it to her, he said, "Thank you, and good day," and turned to leave.

Uncle John quickly stood. "Excuse me, please, but are you actually from the President's office?"

"Yes, sir. President McKinley himself sent me," the man said confidently.

"Would you care to stay and rest awhile?" Uncle John asked. "It's a long way to Washington."

"Thank you, sir, but I have a coach waiting for me outside," the man answered. "Thank you again, and good day."

Liza showed him to the door, and Mandie just stood there holding the envelope. Uncle John put his arm around her and said, "Quick! Open that envelope before all these people die from a heart attack."

Mandie nervously ripped open the flap of the envelope. Carefully, she pulled out a matching cream-colored sheet of paper and unfolded it. She read it silently as Uncle John looked over her shoulder.

Instantly her eyes widened and her mouth opened. "President McKinley has invited me to the White House," she squealed.

"Read it to us," Elizabeth urged.

"It says . . . it says . . . it says . . ." Mandie stammered as she looked at the piece of paper. "It says,

Miss Amanda Shaw
Franklin, North Carolina

I would be most honored with your presence at my forthcoming inauguration for my second term as President of the United States on March 4, 1901. I have heard with much delight of the hospital you are building for the Cherokee Indians and would enjoy hearing personally about it. I look forward to seeing you here on March 1, in time to get acquainted before the ceremonies take up my time.

With best regards,
William McKinley

Mandie just stood there, holding the piece of paper, unable to absorb the message. Uncle John gave her a little squeeze and led her to the settee to sit by her mother.

Suddenly everyone was talking at once.

Uncle Ned leaned over from the chair beside her and patted her hand. "Papoose, Cherokee proud," he said.

"Thank you, Uncle Ned," Mandie replied, smiling up at him. Then, when the message finally soaked in, she could hardly contain her excitement. "Mother, will you let me go to see the President? Please!"

"I am eager for you to visit the President, of course, Amanda, but I wouldn't be able to travel since the baby will be due not long after that," Elizabeth replied.

Mandie instantly turned to her uncle. "Uncle John, will you go with me, please?"

Uncle John shook his head slowly. "No, I'm sorry, Amanda. I have to stay with your mother to see that everything is all right."

Mandie looked over at Mrs. Taft. "Grandmother, can you go with me?"

"I'm sorry, Amanda, but you know I'm planning an extended trip to Europe beginning in February," she reminded her. "I really am sorry, but other people are going with me, and I couldn't change my plans."

Mandie jumped up and waved the note around in the air. "Do you mean the President of the United States invites me to visit him, and I have to say I can't go?"

The adults looked at each other in dismay and shook their heads.

Elizabeth looked concerned. "Amanda, I believe your school exams for that quarter are in March, too, aren't they?" she asked. "You would miss a lot of time from school."

Mandie didn't answer.

Dr. Woodard cleared his throat. "I'd like to know how the President of the United States found out about that hospital being built for the Cherokees," he said.

"I wonder if he also knows about the gold we found in a cave to pay for building it?" Joe asked.

Mandie sat back down on a nearby footstool. How could she miss out on a chance to talk face-to-face with the President of the United States? She had been studying about President McKinley in school, but she never dreamed she would ever receive a handwritten note from him, much less an invitation to visit him.

She tried to fight back the tears, but soon they started rolling down her cheeks as she sat there, holding the letter. She knew the forthcoming baby would prevent her mother and Uncle John from going with her. She tried hard not to get angry.

Uncle John squatted beside her and put his arm

around her. "Cheer up," he said. "We'll figure out something."

Mandie dried her eyes. "But there is no way for me to go," she said. "I can't go alone."

"Never give up hope about anything, Amanda," Uncle John told her.

But there didn't seem to be any reason to have any hope.

When Mandie went to bed that night, she was worried. She knew she would have to send a reply to the President in a few days. And there were so many things against her going that she didn't really think she had much of a chance.

Nevertheless, after Hilda was asleep, Mandie got out of bed and knelt by the window. Looking up at the twinkling stars, she appealed to God. "Please, dear God, please let me go to Washington. Please help us figure out some way for me to go."

As she crawled back into her warm bed, she felt sure that if God wanted her to meet the President, she would find some way to get there.